THE
UNEXPLAINABLE

Jana Nolan

THE UNEXPLAINABLE

Jana Nolan

Earth Star Publications
Cedaredge, Colorado

FIRST EDITION
First Printing March 2017

ISBN 978-0-944851-51-7

Printed in the United States of America

INTRODUCTION

For those of you who aren't familiar with my style of writing, or haven't read any of my books, I would like to say that this one was a real challenge for me to write.

I grew up in a town called Montrose, Colorado. Being a country girl, many of my stories revolve around country living or a small town atmosphere.

The title, *The Unexplainable*, was chosen by me because of the stories themselves. With all the mysteries of the world that we are faced with each day, I take you in a new direction of wondering whether any of this could actually happen in our time period of life.

Sit back and enjoy these stories that will give your thoughts a ride of a lifetime. After reading them, remember that this book is only fiction, or is it?

The first story, "The Unknown Road Going Nowhere," is about a young woman who, after many years of devastation and wrong choices, decides to change her life and travel in a different direction to an unknown place where she hopes she will find a better life, with joy and not pain. In a new town she finds more than she expected and a mystery that challenges her mind of seeing and believing.

The second story, "Shadows in the Night," is about a man who ends up in a city a long ways from where he lived, needing a new start and not knowing that this new start for his life could end his life, because of the danger from three men who are up to no good.

The third story, "The Antique Clock," is about a man and his wife who find out that an item they bought has a history behind it, and that it is capable of just about anything.

The fourth story, "Is He or Isn't He?" is about a woman who meets a man she isn't sure about, and continues to wonder about.

The fifth story, "Check In, But Can't Check Out," is about two young women who defy their parents' wishes and travel to different places they have dreamed about. When danger comes from a place they could never expect it to, they find themselves wondering what to do to avoid it.

As with all of my books, I try to give my readers a lesson of what can maybe happen to them on any day. Fact or fiction?

Now that I have shared with you a brief summary of what each story is about, it is up to you, the reader, to decide if any of these tales are capable of happening at any given moment, or if they are just something that an author such as myself completely made up to captivate her readers.

However you interpret the book, remember that there are strange happenings every day that surround us, or out of bad choices we find ourselves in the middle of. With all of this in mind, enjoy the fictional stories that will make you think.

Jana Nolan

CONTENTS

PART 1
The Unknown Road Going Nowhere

PART 2
Shadows in the Night

PART 3
The Antique Clock

PART 4
Is He or Isn't He?

PART 5
Check In, But Can't Check Out

THE UNKNOWN ROAD
GOING NOWHERE

— 1 —

The End of a Bad Choice

A tall blonde-haired woman in her late 30's, with a sad but relieved look on her face, walked down the long cement stairs of an old courthouse that had been used for the last 70 years and led to the street where she had parked her expensive Corvette convertible.

This day she had sat in the courthouse for several hours, looking at the clock on the wall, wondering how time flies by quickly when no one is ready for it to. But then it drags when something as important as this day was to her.

Rubbing her wrists and hands, trying to sit patiently, she saw her attorney come out of the elevator doors. He was a short, stocky-looking man wearing a brown suit with a tie that looked like it had come from a thrift store. In a nutshell, he wasn't the most expensive attorney in the city, but one who was admired by many people as a fighter in court when needed.

The woman stood up to greet him, and the attorney grabbed the young woman's arm to escort her to her seat in the courtroom. Soon after, a tall, young-looking man stood at the door with his attorney, waiting to make a grand entrance. This man was her soon-to-be ex-husband.

As he walked past the young woman, he gave her a slight smile and nodded his head at her. He had already been advised by his attorney to refrain from rude gestures after entering the courtroom. The man's attorney was dressed in a high-dollar black suit with a tie on that looked like it came from Macy's Department Store. The woman could see that he was a well paid hotshot attorney who only the rich could afford.

Before the judge entered the room, the woman turned her head to look at her husband of twenty years. He saw her looking and again gave her a sideways smile that suggested that he was there to win, as he was convinced that the judge would rule in his favor and she wouldn't get a dime out of him. The woman thought that maybe his attorney might have paid off the judge, and once again he would get everything he wanted.

When the judge entered the courtroom, everyone stood up. As the judge started talking, the woman's thoughts turned to years ago, when she had been a senior in high school and thought that she could have a good life with him, in spite of things that had happened before they were married.

She was a cheerleader and he was a football jock whom all the girls wanted to date. And even though he smiled at other girls, she believed that he was true and faithful to her. They would stand out on the football field after a game, holding each other, talking about their plans to be together after their senior year ended, and repeatedly spoke of their love for one another.

One night after a game, the young man took her home, insisting that he had to leave because his parents were having a big family gathering. He was expected to be there, all dressed up in his tux and sitting at the long oak table. The young man's parents were very rich, and with him being their only child, they knew that he would do exactly as they told him to do, if he wanted all of their money after they passed away.

The young girl and boy came from two different worlds. He was wealthy and she came from a family that had certain values in life, enough money to get by on, lots of love, and a simple lifestyle.

When graduation night arrived, the young man proposed to the young girl and swore that nothing would keep them apart. The young woman said she would marry him and that she knew that they would have a great life together, in spite of the differences that they had.

Months went by, and he started making excuses as to why he had canceled their dates, and why he was always late picking her up when he did show up.

One night, the young woman was curious and went to stand outside the mansion where her fiancé lived. She waited for him to come out the door. Before he could, a car pulled up into his driveway. A beautiful older woman got out. Soon after, the young man came out the door to greet her at her car. They got into her fancy car and drove away.

This was devastating for the young woman, who trusted him with everything she felt inside herself. Running and crying, she ran home. When she opened the front door, she ran past her parents, sobbing so hard that they couldn't understand anything that she said.

Her father went to her room to talk to her, and when he heard about what the young man had done to her, he forbade her to see him again.

The next morning, the young man saw the young woman walking and pulled his car over to the curb of the street. The young woman kept walking, and soon the young man was running after her. She started crying and told him what she had seen. He told her that the older girl was his cousin from a different town, and had come to visit for a few days.

Unfortunately, the young girl believed him and accepted his lies. They talked about running away together, so that there wouldn't be any problems with their families. The young woman agreed that this would be for the best, and within a few days they got married in a small town outside of where they lived.

At this time, the young woman believed she had done the right thing and that she was going to have nothing but a wonderful life with her new husband ... forever. As time went on, the two families accepted their marriage and things appeared to be going well. Shortly after that, her husband started staying out late at night and not coming home until early morning. She would wait up for him, watching out the bedroom window at times.

One night, as she stood at the window, she noticed a car pulling up with an older woman behind the wheel. She got out of her car and went to the passenger side. When she opened the car door, the other woman and the younger woman's husband appeared to be drunk. As the young woman continued to watch out the bedroom window, she saw her husband kissing this other woman that had brought him home.

When he entered the house, he took off his tie and suit jacket and slung them across the couch. He then asked his wife what was for supper.

When the young woman asked him where he had been and why this woman had brought him home, he became enraged. He started throwing things and scream-ing at her that he was tired of how he always needed to explain himself, and that he would do whatever he wanted. And if she didn't like it, she could get out.

The young woman sat down in the chair with her head between her hands, crying and sobbing. In her mind, she had realized that she had married a womanizing liar who could not be trusted again.

Not wanting to face her parents to tell them that they were right about her husband, she continued to play the part of a good housewife who stayed at home and had a hot meal waiting for him when he decided to walk through the front door.

This went on for years, until his temper grew worse

as he wanted more from her. She started to refuse him as she wasn't going to be the second choice, or second woman, that he had gone to bed with that night. With her denying him, he would pick up anything that was close to him and start hitting her with it.

When she went to the store, she had neighbors who would question her about her bruises and black eyes. She always made excuses about her running into things or falling down.

One night in December, just before Christmas, he came home mad. He screamed at her and told her that she was either going to stop telling the neighbors about what he did to her, or else. It scared her and she ran for the door. He opened it as she got to it, and pushed her outside, causing her to slip on the ice and hit the cement sidewalk.

She grabbed her arm, feeling pain, and went next door to the neighbor's house, who then called 9-1-1. That night the police officer took her husband to jail. He was right where he deserved to be.

The young woman packed a bag and left the house. She didn't want to be there when he returned home. She knew that his family, with all of their money, would bail him out, and she wanted a better life than what he was giving her.

The woman remembered and relived this in her mind as she sat in the courtroom that day. She had been abused for years and he was no longer the nice boy from high school. He was an evil, womanizing, abusive jerk that she hoped would pay for what he had done to her physically and mentally.

When the judge sat down, he looked out into the eyes of both the man and the woman, and he told them that he had reviewed everything that had been presented to him by both of their attorneys and had come to a decision. If they had a dispute about his decision, they had the option of discussing it amongst themselves and their attorneys, and he would be the one to decide if it was acceptable in his courtroom.

The young woman looked at her husband and gave him a sideways smile, to let him know that she was ready to accept what the judge had to say. At that moment, she noticed a sweat bead form on his face, and she knew that his cocky attitude was changing.

When the judge started talking, he brought up the charges of mental and physical abuse that the woman had endured for many years. He mentioned that all of this had been reported in the past, and that none of this had been presented before him. It was as if the man and his attorney had attempted to hide the evidence in hopes that the verdict would go in the man's favor.

He then talked about the property and money involved, and that he would make sure that in his courtroom there would be a fair hearing, and not one the local newspaper would print as being a big joke. After he adjusted his seating, he looked once again out at the woman. He then asked her attorney if he had anything he would like to say.

The woman's attorney said, "No, your honor. We think the evidence presents itself."

Then the judge looked at the man's attorney and asked the same question. This time, his attorney stood up and said, "Your honor, my client wants to add that he is very sorry for any abuse that he did in the past. The property and money came from his well-to-do family, and he feels that it is only right that he continue to have it in his possession. We are asking you to please think about this before making your decision on the settlement."

The judge shook his head and told the man's attorney that he had spent several hours going over the papers of why the woman thought that she was entitled to a settlement. He said that he had also reviewed his client's paper work, and was going to administer his decision in a fair way as he was authorized by the State of Colorado.

When the woman turned her head again to look at

her husband, she could see that he had his head looking down at the table with more sweat pouring off of him. This was when he knew that he was in serious jeopardy of losing everything that his family had given him.

She turned her head once again to look at the judge, and waited for him to speak again. Should she feel sorry for her husband of twenty years? Her thoughts were *NO*, as he had lied to her from the beginning, and with all the womanizing he had done over the many years, and the bruises that he had put on her, she felt no remorse. She wanted him to pay for each and every time he had hit her and made her feel insecure as a woman and a person with his roaming eyes for other women and not her.

The judge cleared his voice and said, "I repeat again that I have given this much thought. It is by me, the Judge of District 51 in the County of Denver, and the State of Colorado, that I think it is only fair that the case in matter be resolved with the property and money being split equally. The property shall be sold, and with this, both parties will split it equally as well. The same pertains to the money. If you disagree with my decision, then you can discuss it, and if there is a good reason why I should change this, I will consider it. Otherwise, the decision stands with the court."

The decision had been made, and when the judge hit his podium with his gavel, the man's attorney stood up, yelling that this was not a fair judgment. Then the woman's ex-husband also stood up, stating that there would be no more talk about it. He would agree with this decision. The judge then said that the two parties were legally divorced and to please leave his courtroom.

The man's attorney argued with him, telling him that he could have changed the decision and that he spoke too soon. The man said that he had places to be and that he would make sure that the woman didn't see a dime of any of his money. The judge couldn't stop him.

After hearing what her ex-husband said, she

thanked her attorney and walked out of the courtroom. She knew that in the court of law there was nothing that her ex-husband could do.

So, sitting in her car, she tied a scarf around her head with the ends of it under her neck, and pulled out into traffic to start her new life. Her attorney would make sure that she got her settlement. Her life had been a whirlwind for many years, and she was looking for a new start in a different place, where there was serenity.

This place that she was looking for was unknown, but at the moment she was so upset, she felt like she was on a road going nowhere.

She was running away from her ex-husband, and the place where she had lived for many years, plus the devastation that she had faced that had led her to the courtroom that day. With this, she was taking the chance of it all blowing up in her face, or even danger up ahead in an unknown surrounding. Her thoughts were that no matter where her journey took her, or the highway that it took her on to get there, it had to be better than the life she had just had.

This woman I have been speaking about is me, Brenda Sparks. I learned at an early age that life doesn't come easy and that there really isn't anything for free. There is a price that we all pay, whether it is with money or just our life itself.

For some people, their life is already in place and paid for the day they are born, like my ex-husband's life. Then others, like myself, are born to grow up with hard knocks that either try to destroy or drive us to the edge of disaster, or we learn that we are the ones to change our current situation and move forward, keeping our heads held high, and accept whatever life throws out at us.

I had been driving for several hours on an interstate heading west. The sun was starting to set and I was exhausted from the day. As I drove past a small sign off the roadway, I saw that there was an exit on the upcoming highway where I could get food and lodging.

I made a right turn and followed the highway to another sign that read, "You have reached the Town of Hope." My thoughts were, *Have I finally found the serenity that I have been looking for?*

— 2 —

Two New Friends

With my feeling that this was a sign letting me know that maybe this was the town I was looking for, where I might find peace and serenity for the first time in a long while—and not just a coincidence—I slowed my car down to look at all the buildings and people that were walking down the sidewalks.

I saw a small café that looked old, just like a lot of the other buildings that I had passed so far. I decided to stop for a while and think about whether I really wanted to stay in the town of Hope. I pulled over to the side of the highway and started walking toward the café. The people that I passed were friendly and appeared to be happy as they smiled and nodded at me when I looked at them.

As I tried to open the door of the café from the outside, someone was pushing from the inside. When the door opened, a nice man said, "I am so sorry. I hope the door didn't hit you. Sometimes I don't know my own strength. I should have thought about the fact that someone might be entering the café as I was exiting it. I will hold the door open for you, to make sure that no one else runs into you."

"That would be very nice, and thank you," I said as I smiled at him.

Once he made sure I was securely inside the café, he shut the door and walked away. He was wearing a uniform that was neatly pressed. I could see that he was an officer in the Army and had served our country for many years as he had a silver oak leaf and the border was gold. He had several medals, ribbons and pins. His jacket was amazing.

I walked to the counter and sat down on a stool. The waitress was filling salt and pepper shakers as well as napkin holders. She stopped what she was doing and, with a pencil tucked in her hair behind her left ear, came over to me.

"Can I get something for you?" she asked.

"Yes, I would like to see a menu, please, and a glass of water," I replied.

The waitress brought me a glass of ice water and a menu. She then turned and walked away.

The café was even smaller than I had imagined from the outside of the building. It was decorated in a style with old pictures of movie stars and singers on the walls, dating back to the '50s. It also had an old jukebox that was playing old love songs that I was picturing my parents dancing to. I felt relaxed, calm, and like I was finally where I needed to be. Maybe not forever, but for now.

The waitress came back and asked to take my order. She filled my glass with more ice water and asked me what I would like from the menu.

"I would like a burger, fries and a chocolate malt, please," I answered.

"Okay, I will be right back with your order," she said.

While waiting, I noticed a young woman who had entered the café who might still be in high school. She was holding onto something that looked to me as if it was a résumé or an application for a job. She handed it to the waitress, who then set it in a square container on the counter.

When the waitress returned, I asked her if she knew if the café was doing any hiring, and was told that they were. My next question was if there was a boarding house with rooms to rent in the town. She again said yes and gave me directions to it.

I finished my meal and as I was paying her, I asked for an application. I wasn't sure how long until the money from the divorce would be available to me and I needed a job. I told her that I would fill it out and bring it back to her in the morning. She told me that was fine and also what time the café opened each day.

This time, while opening the front door of the café, I stepped to the side. Apparently that is what the people do here in town, to keep from getting hit by the door.

I walked across the street to my car, still watching the small town of people as they went about their way. I was starting to feel even more like I was a part of this town.

When I drove away to find the boarding house, I noticed about a block away a small group of people who had gathered in one spot to talk. These people weren't smiling and looked very serious about something. Maybe they were discussing an accident that had taken place on the highway, or the schools, or hard telling what. I wasn't going to be concerned about it for the moment.

When I reached my destination for the night, I parked my car and walked up a few steps to the boarding house door. It was dark with no yard light turned on. My thoughts were that they weren't expecting any more people needing a room for the night.

After opening the door, there was a woman standing next to the light switch. She was about to turn it off when she saw me at the door. She smiled and said, "Can I help you, young lady?"

"Yes, you can. My name is Brenda Sparks and I need to rent a room from you for a few days. I am new in town and need a place to stay."

"Well, then, we need you to fill this paper out. I will get you the key to your room," she said as she reached for a key that was hanging on a board behind the desk.

"It is seven dollars a night here, Missy. We have two bathrooms, one for the men and one for the ladies. There are new towels furnished to you every day. You will need to supply your toiletries, and we will also give you new clean sheets each day for your bed. We don't allow smoking in here, or cooking. Each day we serve supper meals at 5:30, and if you miss one, then we will allow you to fix yourself a sandwich from the kitchen area. Not every one of our guests have the same working hours. We allow visitors in the rooms for a short period of time each day, but not to spend the night, unless you pay extra," she explained to me.

"I understand all the rules, and you won't have any trouble out of me," I told her. I paid her the money for three days and walked away, thanking her for letting me stay there.

After walking up the stairs to my room, I could see that the steps were rickety, just like the old building, but I was thankful for a bed to sleep in.

The woman was very nice, but firm about what they expected out of the people that stayed here. I chuckled for the first time in a while. Even with all the rules of the boarding house, and the old rickety stairs in the building, it felt peaceful to me.

Being too tired to fill out the application, I waited. I needed a restful night of sleep.

As birds chirped outside my window, I opened my eyes and, as the country folk would say, I slept like a log. I was awake and ready for my day. It didn't take as long to complete the application as I thought, and I was ready to leave there and search the town, to see more of what I couldn't see last night.

My first stop was to walk to the café. When I entered it, I noticed that they had a big breakfast crowd. I had done some waitressing in high school, so I knew how to do this job. I walked to the counter and the waitress came over to me.

"I'm here to return this application to you," I said. "As you will see, I am not a complete stranger when it comes to working in a restaurant or a café."

The waitress took it from me and reviewed it herself. Then she looked at me and told me to stay there, that she would be right back. I stood there, and within minutes she returned with a smile. She told me that she had run it past the owner and he would like for me to work for him. She said that they opened at 6:00 every morning and that I wasn't needed to start work until the next Monday, which would be in two days. This extra time would give me the opportunity to discover and decide for the last time if the town of Hope was right for me.

I thanked her for the job and walked across the floor to leave the building. I wasn't sure what direction I was going to take first, but saw many shops to the right of me that looked like places of interest. There were many clothing and antique shops. I wanted to check out each one of them. This was something that Denver didn't have with their big shopping malls and outlet stores. Each store had a small bell above the door, to let the people who worked there know when a person had entered. This, to me, was very unique, and again I smiled with excitement.

As I made my way to a clothing store, I decided to go in and take a look. When I opened the door, I saw the same man who had met me at the front door of the café. This time he wasn't dressed in uniform and had a young woman with him, who appeared to be the same one who had come to the café last night, to give them a résumé or an application. This tall, good-looking man noticed me and turned around to smile at me.

I smiled at him, and both the soldier and the young woman walked over to me.

"Hello," the soldier said, smiling back at me. "My name is Mark Holmes. This is my daughter, Kayla. You must be new to this town. I haven't seen you before."

"Yes, I am new. This is the second day of my arrival. My name is Brenda Sparks. I came from a city called Denver in the state of Colorado, and really like your small town of Hope," I responded.

"Our town is not real small, but nothing like the city that you have come from. You are quite a ways from there."

"I noticed last night that you were wearing an Army uniform. I am assuming that there is an Army post close by."

"Yes, just a ways out of town. It is not far from the big mountain that you can see from town. If you would like, someday I can show it to you," Mark said as he smiled again.

"I would like that, Mark," I replied.

I turned to the young girl. "So you are Kayla. I think I saw you in the café last night, returning what appeared to be a résumé or an application to the waitress at the counter."

"Yes, I was in there returning one for school. I have a business education class that I have to take, and they are trying to prepare us for next year, when we either get a job, or go to college. This part of it was filling out applications everywhere in town. I really don't need to work. The basket that the waitress put mine in is actually for my teacher to examine and review, to see if I filled each question out correctly," Kayla explained to me.

"That's nice. It is good experience for you and the other students to know what questions are on an application when you are looking for work."

"Brenda, my dad—even though he tries—has no taste when it comes to women's fashions. Is there a way that I can talk you into staying in here long enough to help me pick out a nice dress for the prom that is coming up?" Kayla asked.

I looked at Mark and he smiled again. This was his way of letting me know that it was okay with him. So I told Kayla that I would be honored to help her. She then took my hand and we walked over to a rack of prom dresses. Mark followed.

Kayla picked out many of which she liked and started for the dressing room. Mark and I stood outside the room and waited for her to come out, modeling each one of them. This went on for an hour of her changing dresses and then coming out of the room, turning around and being an excited teenager. With most of them, I nodded my head yes and looked at Mark.

On the last dress she picked out, she came out of the room, turning around, and when I looked at Mark, he was shaking his head no, just like I was. We both laughed and she laughed as well. I didn't really know Mark, but I was convinced that he wouldn't let her wear it outside the house, let alone to prom. Kayla had found one that she really liked and looked nice in, so we were done.

Both Kayla and Mark were finished in the store, and I, too, was ready to leave. We left at the same time with Mark being the perfect gentleman and holding the door open for not just me, but his daughter as well.

"Brenda, we would love for you to come to our home later, to eat supper with us. It is spaghetti night. Kayla always fixes more than we can eat. Will you do us the honor of joining us?"

"Of course, Mark. It would be my pleasure to dine with both of you. What time would you like me to be there?" I asked.

"I would love to come and pick you up, Brenda. Where are you staying?"

"I am staying at the boarding house for now, Mark, and that would be very nice of you to do this for me."

"Okay, Brenda, I will be there at seven to get you."

"Okay, and thank you. I will see you then," I replied.

I watched them walk away and decided that it was a good opportunity to take the time to drive around and check out more of the town of Hope.

As I was walking back to the boarding house to get my car, I noticed a group of high school boys standing against a car, smoking and talking amongst themselves.

They looked to be about Kayla's age. How little did I know that this wouldn't be the last time I saw them.

I saw a small soda shop and, coming from the city and being unfamiliar with this sort of thing, I went inside to buy something to drink.

Once again, like the old style of the café, I noticed the décor was dated back to the '40s, '50s and '60s.

As I sat on the stool, resting my arms on the counter, an older man approached me to take my order. Everything they had listed to buy was written on a chalkboard across from the counter. I had heard my mother brag about the vanilla sodas that she had bought as a kid, so I decided to try one.

"Can I take your order?" the older man asked.

"Yes, please, I would like a vanilla soda."

I sat there, watching him make it, and was quite impressed by how they were made.

The man brought it to me and I sat there, sipping it. While doing this, I overheard a couple of men talking. In their conversation they mentioned some kind of disturbance or project that the Army post was either working on or involved in. Unfortunately, I had no idea what they were talking about.

"Albert, what is new with all the commotion about the ordeals of what the military are doing now?" a man, who was referred to as Henry, asked.

"I'm not sure, Henry, but from all the talk around town, it has everyone in an uproar. It's hard telling what it could turn out to be."

"This is true, Albert. George Jacobs told me that some of his cows managed to find a way through the fence the other day. When George drove up the road of the mountain, ignoring the 'no trespassing' signs posted, looking for them, he got so far and then got told by a military guard that he couldn't go any further. He said he turned his truck around and started down the road toward his house. After driving for a while, he saw his cows in a distance, lying on the ground. He said their hide was torn clean off of them, and they looked like plucked chickens. Now everyone that has animals are keeping an extra close eye on them."

"What did George think caused this?"

"He has a suspicion, but doesn't know for sure. Some people want to blame this on the military, but then again, if they are involved, how could they have done this bizarre act, and what would they accomplish doing it?" Albert replied.

As I listened to this conversation, and my being new to the area, I felt it was in my best interest to not ask questions or let on that I even heard them speaking. I didn't give it much thought as even living in the city, I heard all about small town gossip and how it can affect people. Also, it was a subject that I wouldn't bring up with Mark.

After finishing my soda, I was on my way back to the boarding house. When I arrived, I climbed in my car, started it, and drove away from the curb to check out the rest of the town and maybe the Army post that Mark had spoken about by the mountain.

That day, the people that I saw walking into stores appeared to be happy, and I could see that many of the stores and buildings had been there for many years. The town looked peaceful to me, unlike what Henry and Albert were speaking about.

My journey that day was going well. I had reached the end of the town, going in the direction of the big mountain, when I passed the Army post. There were many military men and women outside, working on vehicles and performing other duties. It appeared to be bigger than what I expected it to be. The closer I got to the mountain, the more road signs were posted. One of them said:

You have reached what has been turned into a

military reservation. Turn around and go back.

DO NOT ENTER

This being the case, I stopped and turned my car around and went back to the highway I had just turned off of. It was starting to get late enough in the day where I needed to get ready for my date with Mark and Kayla.

Being excited about my dinner invitation and new friends that I had already made, I was ready for an evening of entertainment and good company.

Right at seven o'clock I heard a knock at the door, and I was sure it was Mark.

"Brenda, you look beautiful. Are you ready to stuff yourself from Kayla's cooking?" Mark asked with a chuckle.

"Yes, Mark, thank you again for inviting me to dinner."

"Then let's go put on the feed bag and enjoy the evening," Mark replied as he held the door open for me. I walked out of my room.

As we drove away from the boarding house, I started the conversation. "It is going to be nice to have a home-cooked meal again."

"When my wife was alive, we would entertain a lot," said Mark. "Since then, Kayla and I stay pretty much to ourselves in our home."

"This question might be too soon to ask—and over-whelming, Mark—but what happened to her?" I asked, wondering if I should have.

"It's been several years since Annie passed away. At the time, Kayla was only six. That day, Annie was taking Kayla to school. We got up late that morning and she had missed the school bus.

"The wind was blowing very hard," he continued. "I told her that I would do it, but she insisted on being the one to take her as she said she had errands to do after she dropped her off at school. She told me that they would be fine, and not to worry because she would be back home soon. I kissed Annie and Kayla goodbye, and went upstairs to shower and dress for the day.

"When I was coming downstairs, I heard an ambulance and fire truck pass by the house. I sat down at the kitchen table, waiting for Annie's return, with a terrible feeling inside me. About an hour later, the sheriff showed up at my door to tell me that a huge tree had fallen from the wind storm. As Annie was driving, it had fallen through the top of the car, and the rescue team found Annie lying over Kayla, to protect her from the tree.

"Annie had passed away from a severe blow to her head and brain. She had saved Kayla's life," Mark said as a tear ran down his cheek.

Seeing this made me feel badly for asking him about her. "Mark, I am so sorry. I shouldn't have asked you that question."

"It's fine that you did, Brenda. I feel as if you are a special lady, and as I said, this happened many years ago. It hurt Kayla as she has grown up without her mom. She has shied away from other women before, but she saw something in you that she really likes. Today, on the way home, she couldn't stop talking about you and how much she likes you. I am grateful that now she has a woman in her life whom she trusts and wants to be around, as it isn't easy being the only parent and playing the part of both dad and mom," Mark replied, this time with a smile.

Even with the slight smile, I could see some sadness in his eyes. He had, like myself, experienced devastation in his life.

"Brenda, why did you choose the town of Hope to stay at?"

"My life wasn't nearly as devastating as what you have experienced, Mark. For many years I was married to a man who loved other women, and became very abusive toward me. To make a long story short for now, the day I came to Hope was the day that our divorce was final. When I saw the name of the town, I decided to stop and see if it was the town that I had been looking for. I need serenity. So far, I believe that I have found it."

"I have been stationed here for many years, Brenda. Even though we have things that we are taking care of with my military life right now, that won't last forever. I feel that you picked the perfect place to make your new home."

We had reached their house, and I couldn't believe my eyes. It was much nicer than any of the other homes I had seen in the town.

Once again, after we had stopped in Mark's driveway, he came to my side of the car to open the door for me. This man was a true gentleman and something that I hadn't experienced for many years.

As we entered the house I was amazed at all the beauty that surrounded the living room. It was filled with nice furniture, including several plaques of recognition for his military service on the mantle of their fireplace. Alongside this was a beautiful picture of Mark, Annie and Kayla. Anyone who looked at this could see the love they had for each other, and how happy they all were. On the wall next to the mantle was a picture of Mark shaking hands with our President. Kayla came out of the kitchen to welcome me to their home. She was excited to see me again as I was to see her.

During dinner we talked, laughed and told stories of our past. None of what I told them was from my life with my ex-husband. Our evening was going better than I expected it to when the phone rang. Mark got up from where he was sitting and walked slowly across the room. It was as if he was expecting the phone call, but didn't want to answer it, for fear of who was calling or what they had to say.

"Yes, General Cox. What did you find out?" There was a brief hesitation of conversation. Then again Mark spoke. "I will be there in a short while. Tell them not to do anything until I get there." Mark hung up the phone and turned to Kayla and me. As he walked across the floor to give Kayla and me the news, I looked at her. She had a look on her face expressing that this was not the first time she had experienced late night phone calls for her dad.

"Kayla, I am sorry, but I am needed at the mountain. It is going to be another late night before I can return, so don't wait up for me. Brenda, I am sorry, but I am needed at the mountain and sorry that I need to cut this wonderful evening short with you. You are welcome to stay here and visit with Kayla for as long as you like, and I am sure that she won't mind taking you back to the boarding house."

"Thank you, Mark. I had a great evening," I replied.

"We did too, Brenda. I would like it if we could all do this again soon."

"Me too," I said.

Mark kissed Kayla goodbye and turned to leave the house. With this, I could see worry on her face, as if she were afraid and wondering if he would return as he had told her he would. My only thought was to stay there awhile and try to get her mind off of her thoughts for the time being.

I took her hand and we walked back to the couch where we were sitting. "What are your plans after graduation, Kayla?" I asked.

"I have hopes of starting UCLA in the fall. I am excited about it, but will miss my dad."

"I am sure you will. He appears to be a great dad."

"Where did you live before you came to Hope?"

"I lived in Denver, Colorado," I replied.

"I've heard a lot about Denver, and it sounds like a good place to live."

"It is very nice there, if the person living there is happy. I wasn't."

"Why weren't you happy, Brenda?" Kayla asked in her soft, sweet voice.

"Let's just say for now that my life there wasn't what I had hoped it would be."

With these words, it seems to pacify her. She was young, and before long she would be on her way to start a new life for herself after graduation, and I didn't think she needed to hear about how my pathetic life had started out —and, because of circumstances and situations, didn't get better.

We continued to talk about little things like her boyfriend as I hung on every word she said. At that moment, I felt like a protective mother. I had known her for only one day, but wanted to listen to every word that she spoke. Kayla, being young and beautiful with very dark black hair like her mother, Annie, whom I'd seen in the picture of the three of them, I knew that there was a good chance that she, too, could get mixed up with the wrong boyfriend as I had. This I didn't want for her.

After an hour of just "her and me" time, I knew that it was getting late. I didn't want Kayla driving me back to the boarding house any later than it was, so I told her that it was time for me to leave.

Our drive back was filled with laughter and more girl talk. When we reached my destination, I climbed out of her car and told her that I'd had a great time and was looking forward to doing it again sometime soon. She also had a good time and was happy that I had come there to dinner. When she drove away, I watched to make sure she was okay. Again, the motherly instinct took over in me.

When I walked into the boarding house, I had no idea what was going on with Mark on the mountain. If I knew, I probably would have understood more of why Kayla had that look on her face when her dad turned to walk out the door.

At the mountain, Mark was inside of it, talking to the General who had called.

"Now what, General? We have tried for days to get them to come out of there peacefully. We aren't really sure how many of them are in there. Before long, I am afraid that more of the townspeople will be coming up here to see what is going on in here. I am not only worried for my daughter Kayla's safety, but also for the safety of everyone in this entire area. If we don't do something soon about the situation, there are going to be more of these things coming here to check on what is already here," said Mark.

"I know exactly what you are saying. If any of what is in here leaks out in town, we will have a riot on our hands, and I am not sure if any of our troops can hold them back, except through force. I have made phone calls and expecting to hear something back soon. We are going to do whatever it takes to keep everyone safe, Mark. Don't worry about Kayla. I know that you are afraid for her life, as of the day you were for Annie's."

"Thank you, General. You are right. I can't lose her as well."

At the boarding house, after I walked into my room, the phone rang. I could see that it was Mark calling.

"Brenda, I was just getting ready to leave you a message. Tomorrow, Kayla and I have plans to picnic somewhere, hike and do some rock climbing. Would you be interested in coming with us?"

"Yes, I would love to go with you. It has been many years since I have done anything like that."

"Okay then, Kayla and I will pick you up tomorrow morning around eight o'clock."

"That sounds fine. Thank you for including me."

This being a nice surprise, I again was ready for an exciting adventure in the morning with Mark and Kayla.

My day was completed, and it was time to go to sleep. I was looking forward to another day of fun with my new friends.

— 3 —
Secrecy and Curiosity

When the sun peeked through my window, I woke up. As I lay in bed, my thoughts were of Mark and Kayla. I was wishing that I had found a man like Mark when I was in high school, and how I should have listened to my mom and dad, and how I should have gone to college instead of believing my ex-husband. So many thoughts of "what ifs," and what I should have done and didn't do for years wasted in my life.

Knowing that I couldn't get any of this time back made me think again that it all had been a lesson learned and that I had the opportunity now to make everything in my life good again. With birds chirping outside the window and the beautiful day ahead of me, I was ready for another day of my new life.

At 8:00 a.m. I heard a knock on my door. Expecting to see Mark standing there, I opened it.

"Good morning, Brenda. Are you ready to live some country life?"

"Yes, I am, Mark. It is going to be a beautiful day today," I replied.

As we walked down the steps of the boarding house, I saw Kayla waiting in the car with a big smile. She had been watching Mark and me as we walked together. From her smile I wondered if maybe she might be playing matchmaker, and I was the one she had chosen to be with her dad, so he wouldn't be lonely when she went away in the fall to college.

Before long I knew that she would want to know more about me and my life, now and in the past. I was prepared to tell her everything, but not now.

The words out of her mouth were, "Good morning, Brenda. I see that everyone is on board now. Let's go have some fun in the sun."

Mark and I just smiled at her and at each other. We were ready for fun and a relaxing day.

Our first stop was back at their home. In the anticipation and excitement of the day, they had forgotten the picnic basket.

As we drove away, Kayla said, "Where to today, Dad? Can we hike up the mountain until it's time to eat?"

"Not today, Kayla. At the moment, civilians aren't allowed up there. The only ones allowed up there are military men and women with a secret clearance. You know that. I can't tell you anything about what is happening there, so don't ask what is going on," Mark responded.

"I won't, Dad. I am very familiar with that answer from you," Kayla said with a slight giggle.

"Instead, we are going to show Brenda the beautiful rock formations not far from here. We can rappel off of them and follow the trails to the other ones."

"That sounds like fun," I said. "I learned how to climb and rappel years ago, when I was in high school, living in Colorado. We have some beautiful rock formations there as well."

As Mark turned off the highway onto a road, I was told that hiking and rappelling were some things that they both loved to do as well. We were on our way to a place that would take me back in time.

It wasn't long and we had reached the destination. Kayla and I got out of the car to help Mark carry all the equipment that we needed. They had brought harnesses, helmets, ropes, spring-loaded cams, nuts, tricams and quickdraws to keep us all safe with the right gear needed to do this.

I was glad I had worn a long-sleeved shirt and jeans, to protect me from the sharp crystals in the cracks. As we climbed the rocks, we placed anchor points that would be permanently fixed to the rocks. Eventually, we made it to the top.

Now it was time to descend back down. All of us had good rope management skills and knew how to tie strong knots that wouldn't come untied. Also, we had rigged the ropes through the rappel device back-up safety systems, like an auto block knot, in case the rappel system failed. A huge plus was that we knew how to retrieve and pull the ropes down from the anchors after rappelling back down the rocks. I hadn't done this in years and had forgotten about the wonderful rush that it gave me each time that I did it.

Doing this had given all of us an appetite. We walked around in search of some trees for shade, so we could eat and rest.

"Thank you so much for including me in this fun day," I told Mark and Kayla.

"It was our pleasure, Brenda," Mark replied.

"You are good at it," Kayla responded.

"I was about your age, Kayla, when I learned how to do this. I would climb to the top of a rock and sit there and think. A writer takes his or her mind in a different direction, and at that time of my life I needed to do the same thing. It always gave me peace."

"You have a very special mind, Brenda," Mark replied as he could see that there was more to me and my past that, for now, I chose to keep silent and hidden deep inside of me.

"Thank you, Mark."

"Thank you for coming with us today. It made Kayla and me very happy to have you with us."

Again, all I could do, or wanted to do, was smile.

We hiked back to the road where the car was and

found a shady tree where we spread a blanket out on the ground, to sit and eat what had been prepared for our picnic. Considering the fact that Annie had been gone since Kayla was six, she had grown up being quite the good cook. After we were done eating, Kayla announced that she was taking her own hike and would not be gone too long.

"Don't go anywhere near the mountain. I know how curious you can get at times," Mark said with a worried tone in his voice.

"I won't, Dad. You keep telling me this. By you doing this, it makes me wonder even more what is going on with the mountain."

"Kayla, I have told you before, many times, that it is top secret. A lot is taking place there right now. It is a military reservation, and as you know, I am a major colonel and with this I am under the gun if I was to share anything with you," Mark told her firmly.

"Okay, Dad. I understand."

After hearing what Mark told her, I thought about what the two men were talking about in the soda shop. There was something that the military was doing up there that appeared to be dangerous. I knew that Mark would have revealed everything to her if he hadn't been sworn to secrecy. I knew that sooner or later, the truth would surface as it always does.

As Kayla walked away, Mark laid down on the blanket. As he looked upward at the sky, he said, "Brenda, do you ever wonder what all is up there that we can't see?"

This seemed to me like an odd question to ask. "Yes, I have wondered many times. I know about the many planets, and at night, when the stars and moon are bright, I have wondered even more."

"Being in the military for as long as I have been, I have found out about many things. With the top security clearance that they gave me, I often go to bed to sleep, but lie there at times with one eye open. Kayla has endured a lot being raised in military life. I wish I could tell her why she isn't allowed on or near the mountain. All I can do is my hardest to keep her safe."

"I am sure in her heart she understands more than you think she does. I can see that she is very proud of you, and what you do."

Mark sat up some on the blanket. He leaned over toward me and it looked like he was about to kiss me, but then he changed his mind and laid back down, then hesitated. He looked at me and said, "Brenda, I hear my car phone ringing. I'll be right back." He quickly got up and ran to his car.

I could see Kayla walking in our direction. She wasn't smiling and, in fact, she looked upset or sad about something. She walked toward Mark and the car. Not being far from them, I stayed where I was. I could hear what was being said.

As Mark answered the phone, he said, "Yes, General, is there something that I need to be aware of? Before I went home last night, we had everything at bay, so that nothing would get out of control after I left there. There were many men who remained to watch everything. As far as I know, no one other than us, and the ones that have been instructed to stand guard, are aware of anything. I was there quite late, and so far today, I haven't gone back there to review what we already know."

There was a slight hesitation as the General was talking. Then Mark said, "I will be turning in my report to you for the President by the end of the week."

Kayla had reached Mark. How much of this conversation did she hear? I knew that all of what he was doing right now was heavy on her mind. She was a young woman with a lot of life to live and learn about. She knew that if she asked him what the phone call was about, she wouldn't find out anyway, so she left it alone and didn't ask. She just stood there, looking at him with sad eyes. Was this because of what she suspected was going on with her dad and the military? Or had she come across something disturbing on her walk?

There was another slight hesitation, and then Mark said, "Okay, General. I will go check things out. You can expect me there as soon as I can get there."

The conversation ended. When Mark turned around, he saw Kayla behind him. With her not knowing everything that he had said, and he not being able to tell her anything, he just looked at her and told her that it was time to leave.

They both walked back toward me, and as we picked up everything to put back into the car, Kayla didn't say a word.

In fact, on the way back into town, no one said anything. I could see that Mark had a lot on his mind. Kayla just kept staring out the window. We'd had a fun day, and it was too bad that it had to end the way it did.

When we arrived at the boarding house, Kayla finally started talking. She asked me if she could come by the café tomorrow and speak with me about something that was on her mind. Of course, I told her yes.

Before they drove away, Mark asked me if I would like him to escort me to my room. I told him that it was still early enough in the day and I was going to walk around town for a while. He told me he was sorry that we had to cut the day short, and said that he had a wonderful time and would like it if he could take me out to dinner soon. My answer to him again was yes.

I watched them drive away, and then I started walking in a different direction of Hope. Once again, I saw the young group of boys I had seen before, and this time they were staring at me. I said hello to them and kept watching at times, to see if, for some reason, they were following me. They were standing against the same old car as before, talking, and it looked like one of the boys was missing from their crowd.

I kept walking and found an antique shop that was

open. I went inside and browsed for some time. When I came out, the boys were gone. I continued to check out other stores that caught my interest, and before I knew it, I was tired, so I went back to the boarding house, wondering what all the commotion was about with Mark, the General and the mountain. Also, I was wondering why Kayla looked so sad as she was walking back to us after taking her walk.

At the mountain, Mark and the General were talking again.

"Mark, I didn't want to do it, but I had no choice. The Staff Sergeant that you left to stand guard wasn't doing his job. A civilian managed to get in here. We are lucky that one of the other soldiers saw him in time. If he hadn't, by now the news of what is here would be all over town. Everyone would have been running up here, and we can't have a riot on our hands. I had no choice but to lock up Mr. Peterson for now, until this is all taken care of."

"I'm sorry, General. I will make sure this doesn't happen again. Since this has happened, I am sure that there could be more men from Hope who are curious and coming up here. Someone here on the post can't be trusted, as I have heard stories from some of the people in town, standing around in a group. At the time, I wasn't wearing my uniform and they had no idea that I am a soldier.

"What we have here is dangerous, and whoever it is that is leaking out information to the people will be caught and punished. As for Mr. Peterson, I agree that you had no other choice but to lock him up for now. Has anyone questioned him this morning?"

"Yes, and he is mad," said the General. "He said he saw a circle on the mountain and walked up here to see what he could find. When he was asked what he saw, the only thing he said was something that a child would say: 'Wouldn't you like to know? I want out of here now.' The Lieutenant told him that his stay in there would be for a while, as he had broken military restrictions and ignored the signs telling him to not go any farther."

"As for his family, what are we going to tell them?" Mark asked.

"The truth. That her husband was caught on military government land, with a no-trespassing sign all over the mountain, and that he disregarded and disobeyed it. That we had no choice but to lock him up, and that he will stand trial for what he did," the General replied.

"They have talked to us, but have they come out yet?" Mark asked.

"No, they are still in there, and if we don't get them out of here soon, it is going to be an all-out war when the others show up to look for them. Every available man here needs to be aware of this and to be prepared for anything and everything," the General said.

"Okay. I will put extra men here to watch what they do next. I am thinking that they will be showing us what they are here for soon."

"Mark, we already know what they are wanting to do here. This is what frightens me. I am going home now. Keep watch and get other men up here today. Also, post them outside and around the mountain. We can't take a chance again of anyone just walking in here," the General instructed.

"Okay, I am on it right now, sir," Mark said with a worried sound to his voice as he knew just how curious Kayla was and how much she loved the mountain. He had to make sure that she didn't see what he was seeing.

I had made it back to the boarding house and was ready to sit down to eat with the other guests that had rooms there. At the table there were some older people who were talking. I was wondering why they were talking very softly. Then again, I was a stranger to them and they weren't comfortable enough with me to include me in their conversation.

"Liza, did you hear anything new that you would like to share with me?" an older lady named Jackie asked.

"I heard that Old Man Peterson didn't come home last night. He told his wife that he was going out to buy some smokes and would only be gone for an hour. She went to the drugstore last night, when he didn't return after three hours, and they hadn't seen him. She said that he had been awful quiet yesterday and she was worried that something had happened to him."

"Really!! So was she going to check the police station, hospital, or the morgue?" the woman called Jackie asked.

"That was her plan," Liza replied, "and I haven't seen her since, so I don't know what she found out."

"Oh my!! I hope he is okay!"

"Me too."

Those were the only words that they spoke until after they ate and walked away from the table.

Hearing what I had heard made me curious like Kayla, and also wondering why the military, or police department, didn't handle whatever was going on around the mountain before now. Regardless, it was time for me to go to bed and get ready for my first day of work the next day. I was calling it a night.

Up early and excited to be working again, I was showered, dressed and out the door a bit earlier than I needed to be, but wanted to make an early appearance to show that I was on time and willing to work. The morning crowd of people were at the café when I arrived. Having experience as a waitress and cook, I would need very little training, if any.

As I was putting on an apron, I overheard another conversation that intrigued me, coming from two younger women.

"Carol, what do you think about all the talk around town?"

"All of it seems far-fetched to me. I don't know what to think," Carol answered back.

"It sounded that way to me as well, until Marla told me she overheard a couple of soldiers talking about a huge

33

circle that was on or around the mountain."

"A huge circle?"

"That's what I am sure she said, and that the mountain was lit up like a Christmas tree a couple of nights ago."

"Did they say what had caused the circle? That sounds too bizarre for me to believe."

"I don't know as Marla didn't say. This is something that the military wants to keep secret, but before long word will get out, and then everyone will know. This is just another example of what our government is hiding from us."

Both ladies got up out of their chairs to walk to the register and pay for their food.

My thoughts turned to Kayla and I wondered if this was what she had heard her dad saying to the General. Perhaps she wanted to talk to me about it, to see if for some reason Mark had told me what was upon or close to this mountain.

My day went forward and ended without seeing Kayla. I was concerned about her and why she hadn't come into the café as planned. My shift was over, so I left there and walked toward the boarding house and then I saw Kayla and a young man talking loudly.

"Jimmy, why did you do this to me?" Kayla yelled out at him.

"You have it wrong, Kayla. Sue Ann made all that up. You know that I wouldn't cheat on you," Jimmy replied.

"Don't keep lying to me. Sunday I was with my family and I went for a walk. I saw your car parked off the old road, and then I saw you and Sue Ann making out!"

"Kayla, you saw wrong. She was in my car, but I saw her walking on the road, so I stopped and asked her if she wanted a ride back to town. Then I got a flat tire and pulled off the road to change it. What you saw was her helping me," Jimmy said as he grabbed her arm to keep her from walking away.

"Oh, she was helping you all right!!" Kayla took her arm and jerked it away from Jimmy's firm grip that he had on it. As she looked up, she saw me standing there. With tears streaming down her face, she said, "Brenda, I was on my way to see you when Jimmy caught up with me."

Jimmy walked away and I said, "It's going to be okay. I am here now."

I took her hand and told her to walk with me to the boarding house, where we could talk in private.

When we entered my room, Kayla continued to sob and cry. I shut the door and said, "Kayla, it is okay to cry. Tears are the cleansing of one's soul."

She needed the comfort that only a mother could give, and even though I wasn't her mother, she looked up to me and I had grown in such a short time to love her. Still sobbing, she said, "How could he have done this to me?"

"Kayla, start at the beginning and tell me everything," I replied as I held her in my arms.

"Yesterday, when you and dad were talking after we ate, I was walking on the road when I saw a car that looked like Jimmy's. Out of curiosity, I walked toward it to see if I was right. It *was* his car."

She continued, "As I got closer, I noticed that Sue Ann, a girl that likes Jimmy too, was sitting in his car next to him and their heads were close together. I started crying and ran as fast as I could until I couldn't run any further.

"I started walking then, and when I got closer, I noticed Dad talking on the car phone again, like he does all the time. I was glad we left there as I was ready to go home to be alone.

"Today at school, I asked Sue Ann why she was with Jimmy, and she told me that they were making out in his car. She confirmed what I thought was happening and suspected. Of course, she told Jimmy that she told me, and he came to find me. Between what Jimmy had done and the top secret that Dad is keeping from me, I don't know what to think or believe anymore," Kayla said with still more tears running down her face.

I took some tissue from the box on top of my night stand and wiped her face to get rid of the tears. Then I said, "Kayla, I know you are upset, and you have every right to be. No girl likes to be cheated on by their boyfriend. I, too, have had a similar disappointment. It started before I was out of high school. Being the leader of the cheer-leading squad, and my boyfriend being a football jock, I, too, believed that he would never hurt me. I was a young girl in love with a cheating, lying, two-faced snake that showed me through time that the only one that I can really count on or trust is myself.

"As for the reason why none of us are allowed near or around the mountain is something that your dad is working out with the military, to make it safe again, and he has been sworn to secrecy and has to follow rules and regulations, or he will get in a lot of trouble. When he took the oath, he was sworn to secrecy and that can't be changed. He would be held responsible through the military and our government if he betrays them," I spoke, still wiping away tears from her eyes and from her face.

"Thank you, Brenda, for comforting me. I have known for many years that Dad is limited to what he can tell me. I also know that with his rank, it is not an easy job. Many nights he has left the house to go on post, or the mountain, for some reason. This has been going on for a while. When I walked down the sidewalks in town, I heard many scared people talking. Even people that live close to the mountain are afraid. They talk in front of me because they don't know who I am, or that my dad is in the military. There is a lot of assuming going on with them," Kayla replied back as she had finally stopped crying.

"I, too, have heard some wild stories. We are both safe or your dad wouldn't keep you here."

"The stories scare me, Brenda," Kayla replied.

"The next time your dad leaves you alone at night, ask him if you can come to the boarding house and stay with me. You are always welcome here. As for your boyfriend, Jimmy, you really need to forget about him. It will be hard to do at first, but worth it in the end. I don't want bad things happening to you as it did to me at your age. It is easier to walk away than to waste your life wanting to believe that things will get better as it only gets worse."

"Again, thank you. I will try hard to follow your advice."

At that moment, I hoped that what I had told her would keep her safe and making the right choices, but from the way she responded back to me, I was afraid that it would take more than one conversation with her to make sure she chose the right path in her life.

Something told me that there was a reason why I was here in Hope. Was it for me, or for Kayla and Mark?

Soon after I had spoken what I wanted to refer to as "words of wisdom" to her, she was ready to leave. I walked her back downstairs and down the steps outside the boarding house. I asked her if she needed a ride home and she responded to me that the walk would do her good, and give her time to think. If I would have known that—hiding in the bushes outside was Jimmy—I would have insisted on taking her home. He had followed us to the boarding house, and now he knew where I lived as well.

— 4 —

Questions and No Answers

The next day at work was busier than the day before. The small café was packed with people talking about the mountain and what they had heard, or believed, to be taking place there. It sounded to me as if the people who lived in Hope, or around it, were ready to storm the mountain and do their best to overtake the military men and women that were placed there for whatever reason.

I listened to what they talked about and knew that it was time to discuss with Mark everything being said, so that he would be aware of all of it. I went to the back of the café to use the phone and called the number Mark had given me. He didn't answer, so I left him a message, letting him know that it was important for him to call me ASAP, or to come to the boarding house when I got off work, so we could talk.

When my day at work ended, I walked back home to wait for a call. About 9:00 p.m. there was a knock at my door. Expecting to see Mark standing there, I opened the door. Instead of Mark, Jimmy had come to pay me a visit.

"I need to talk to you, lady," Jimmy said with his foot firmly placed inside the doorway, just enough to where I couldn't close it.

"What do you want, Jimmy?" I asked with a scowl on my face.

"I want to know why you are pumping Kayla with words telling her to stay away from me. Lady, you have no idea what I am capable of!" Jimmy replied harshly.

"What I witnessed was uncalled for. You were holding Kayla to keep her there, so she wouldn't walk away. I know a man that did the same thing to me when he was a boy like you, and if I can spare Kayla from all the drama and pain from a sleaze-bag like you, I am going to do it," I said with a firm tone to my voice.

"Lady, you need to mind your own business. At that point, you and I will get along fine."

"Jimmy, I have no fear. If you are trying to frighten me, it isn't working. Now get your foot back where it belongs and leave here now!"

"I warned you!" Jimmy said as he moved his foot and walked away, looking back at me. In my mind he was a punk, just like my ex-husband was. I shut the door and locked it.

When I walked back to the chair in my room, waiting for either a call or a visit from Mark, the phone rang. It was him.

"Thank you for calling me back, Mark."

"Brenda, every time I speak with you is a pleasure. What's up?"

"Thank you for saying this. I have to see you to discuss some matters that concern you, and something else that I feel like you should be aware of," I said.

"Okay, that can be arranged. I am pretty much tied up tonight and at home, awaiting the General's arrival. I can pick you up for dinner tomorrow night if you like, and then we can have plenty of time to talk about whatever it is that you want to talk about."

"That would be fine," I said as I smiled at the phone, and thought that the word *yes* was becoming a big part of my vocabulary when it came to Mark.

"Okay then, I will pick you up tomorrow night about six o'clock. This will give us plenty of time to visit," Mark replied.

We said our good-nights and it was time for me to

call it a day. I knew that when I spoke to him that I had to make my words perfectly clear and let him know exactly what was said in the café today. Also what was going on with Kayla, so he could know that Jimmy was very intent on getting her to take his side of their conversation that they'd had the other day, and also that he wouldn't give up on her that easily. I closed my eyes and soon I was asleep.

Up early again and ready for a long day, I had a paper to mail to my attorney, giving him my new address as to where to send me what he needed to, so I left my room and went to the small post office before going to work.

When I walked through the front door of the café, it was again interesting. There was even more talk and speculation about what the military was planning or doing day and night, at or on the mountain. Everyone had their own version of the reasoning behind all the secrecy that was being withheld from them. I hadn't lived in Hope that long and had no opinion or knowledge about it. That day I had acquired many stories to tell Mark. My mind was exhausted from everything I had heard, but I was prepared for the dinner date and conversation.

Later in the afternoon, the activity at work had slowed down. People coming and going were less talkative and somewhat too quiet. It was as if they were all thinking about something that they were afraid could harm all of us and were inevitably waiting for something to fall out of the sky.

When my day at the café was over, I was leaving and when I opened the door to go outside the building, I noticed the same teen-aged boys standing across the street against a hot rod. They were wearing jeans, white tee-shirts with a pack of cigarettes rolled up in the sleeves of the shirt, with arms crossed. It looked like a film clip from the '50s or '60s.

Their eyes were focused on me. In the middle of all the boys stood Jimmy. He and his punk friends were there to try to scare me, and it wasn't working. All of this with them was a piece of cake compared to the way my life had been before I came to Hope.

I walked out the front door, heading in their direction. As I passed them I smiled and said, "Nice try, boys." I kept walking, and before I was too far away to hear them speak, I overheard one of the boys say, "It didn't work, Jimmy. That lady wasn't afraid and I won't get into trouble because of you. If you want Kayla back, this isn't the way to go about it," the smartest boy out of the bunch said.

By then I had walked too far away to hear what Jimmy replied back to him. I wasn't going to stop to hear it as I had a date to get ready for.

While walking back to the boarding house, I couldn't help but notice men and women who had gathered in the street who were still talking about the mystery that the people in town were obsessed about. I would be in denial if I didn't admit that I, too, was concerned and wondering what this was all about, and what the outcome would be. I also wanted to know what it was that had so many people scared to death.

As I passed an older man with gray hair and a gray beard, mumbling, I heard him say, "Apocalypse is near, young lady." For some weird and scary moment I was asking myself if he was right. Should I be terrified as well?

At 6:00 p.m., expecting to hear Mark's knock at the door, I sat in my room when the phone rang. "Mark, is that you?" I said as I answered the phone.

"Yes, Brenda, it's me. I am going to need a couple more hours before I can pick you up. I got another call from the General and I am needed back at the mountain."

"Is everything okay there?" I asked.

"I will know for sure when I get there. I am looking forward to our dinner later."

"Me too. Don't worry, I won't ask any more questions as I know you can't answer them," I said with a giggle.

"Thank you, Brenda, and you have to know that if I

could, I would tell you and Kayla everything."

"I know you would and it's okay. I will see you soon," I said as I hung up the phone.

Now it was the waiting game, so I sat there thinking about all the words that were said today from different people in the café, and then the words from the old man after work. I also was thinking about something that I hadn't shared with Mark or Kayla. This was that my own father had been in the military. I knew firsthand what it was like growing up, moving around from one country or state to another and not staying in any one place too long. I also knew about security as my father was a captain and many times I heard the same speech about him telling me, "Don't ask me any questions as I am sworn to secrecy."

Whether it be military life or civilian life, a person's life in the real world should be an open book, but because of devastation, betrayal and disappointment, life has a way of showing us that sometimes things are better left unsaid, and this way no one other than the person living or who lived their life gets hurt.

For some people it takes a short time to learn this, and for others it takes their whole life.

The other day, when Mark and I had lain on the blanket talking, I felt as if he wanted to break the rules and let me know information he wasn't allowed to say. Whatever this turned out to be, I had learned a long time ago to expect anything and everything, as life is full of surprises, whether they be good or bad.

I continued to go over bits and pieces in my mind, reliving my entire life, when I heard a knock at my door.

I was happy to see Mark when I opened the door. It was time to relax my mind until we had our conversation, which I was sure would come later in the night.

Mark said, "Brenda, I am sorry for making you wait and showing up later than was planned."

"Everything is good," I replied.

"Let's go eat. I am starving and sure that you are as

well. Later, after dinner, we can talk about what you want me to know."

"All of this works for me, and I am ready."

After making sure that I was in the car and closing my door, Mark got in and we drove away. Again I could see that Mark was in deep thought and that whatever he was thinking about was something serious.

When we reached the restaurant, there were more cars there than I had expected for as late as it was. As we pulled into the parking lot, Mark turned off the engine and came around once again to open my door and let me out. He was a true gentleman.

There appeared to be a car loaded with high school boys sitting not far from where we had parked that had arrived about the same time that we did. The difference was that we got out of the car to walk into the restaurant, and they didn't. Maybe we had been followed by Jimmy and his gang.

When we were inside and had gotten seated, the waitress came to bring us a menu and water.

As the waitress walked away, Mark said, "You look very nice tonight. I am happy you called me as I wanted to take you to this restaurant."

"This place is very nice. For such an old town, I didn't know that a place like this existed. Thank you for bringing me here," I replied.

"Again, Brenda, it is my pleasure. There are a lot of buildings in Hope that look old and run down, but when you enter them, they have been remodeled."

We looked through the menus and waited for the waitress to return. As we waited for her, we talked about everything except what I had called him about that needed said. When the waitress did come to take our orders, we were ready and—as Mark had put it earlier—starved.

It was starting to be quite late in the day. Our time together always went faster than I wanted it to. I knew better than to expect too much, and because of all the bad choices and mistakes that I had made in the past, I wanted to not let my emotions get out of control again. We ate and were ready to leave.

When we walked out the door of the restaurant, I looked around the parking lot. After we had entered the establishment, no one else walked through the door. This was again a thought as my mind went into overdrive. Was that Jimmy's car, and were those boys watching us, to make sure that we entered the restaurant so that he could pay Kayla a surprise visit and talk to her again?

I wasn't sure that she had told her dad the same story she had told me, and if she hadn't, it was time that he knew what Jimmy had done and might do again to her.

I glanced out the side mirror of the car, to see if we were being followed, and it didn't appear to be that way. After reaching the boarding house and entering my room, it was time for us to talk.

"You sounded on the phone as if there is something that you are really concerned about. Please tell me what it is," Mark said.

With a slight hesitation, I replied, "Yes, I do have something that I feel as if you should be aware of. Every day on the sidewalks, or in the café, there have been many people talking about all the activity at the mountain. The people here are very afraid. I overheard someone saying that the people in town need to storm the mountain, to see what the military is hiding. A man on the street believes that the end of the world is near.

"Some ladies were saying that a man disappeared and didn't make it home one night. His wife was terrified that something bad had happened to him. I know that you are not allowed to tell anyone anything, and can't share information with Kayla or myself, and I understand this more than you think, as I grew up as well being a military child. My dad was a captain in the Army. We traveled all over the world like you and Kayla have done. By the time I was in high school, my dad was old, cranky and tired of all the hoops he had to jump through each and every day in military life, so he retired.

"It wasn't long when he took up drinking to get through each day. He would tell me that he was on an unknown road going nowhere during his military years, as the secrets he had to keep inside were secrets that he wanted to shout out to the world, but couldn't. He said the only way he could sleep at night was to drink during the day and at night. He also said that when he closed his eyes at night, he could see all the different things that he couldn't talk about, and it was more than he could endure.

"I haven't known you long, Mark, but sometimes when I look into your eyes, I see that you are struggling with something, and you—like my dad—want to tell the world what is hidden deep inside of you that you will carry to your grave, as my dad will do because of what he has seen and been told."

"Everything that you feel about me is true, Brenda. I, too, wish I could shout out everything that I am carrying inside to the world. I know that everyone with a secret clearance feels this way as well. Thank you for telling me about some of your life. I felt a connection to you the moment I saw you standing outside the café that night that you came to Hope.

"I feel there is a reason why we kept seeing each other in awkward places. Yes, I, too, have many secrets hidden inside of me for many years. I have tried very hard to not let any of them affect Kayla, and my wife Annie, when she was alive. I have good days and bad ones. As far as me deciding to take up drinking when I retire, I really don't see that happening to me. Everyone handles things differently in their lives. I am sorry your dad chose this path, and that you went through this with him.

"As for all the talk around Hope, we are already aware of it. In fact, some of the people who live here thought they could go up the mountain to see what we are doing up there. Most of them have been sent home in a rage, and so some of what you have heard is probably far-fetched.

"I have noticed something about Kayla. She has been very quiet lately and, for her, this is unusual. She has always been my little chatterbox. Other than her being a teenager and her emotions running wild, have you noticed a problem that I am not aware of?"

"Yes, there is something else that you should be aware of. I noticed Kayla's sadness the afternoon she went hiking, and after she came back from her walk. I watched her walk up to you when you were talking to the General on your car phone. She kept staring out the car window when you were taking me home. When she asked me if it would be all right to come talk to me the next day at the café, I thought that she might have overheard your conversation with the General, and thought maybe you might have told me something about the mountain and not her. I waited for her all day to show, and she didn't.

"When I walked out of the café, she was having a heated conversation with her boyfriend, Jimmy. It appears that Jimmy was parked off the side of the old road that leads to the mountain, and Kayla saw him in his vehicle with a girl by the name of Sue Ann. According to Kayla, they had their heads together. On the street, Kayla was trying to get away from him and he had her by the arm and wouldn't let her leave, telling her that what she saw was not what it appeared to be, and that he had just stopped to give Sue Ann a ride, and because he had a flat tire shortly after he picked her up. Kayla kept telling him that he was lying to her and to stop, because Sue Ann had told her everything. Again he kept insisting that she was wrong and that nothing had happened with Sue Ann.

"She saw me standing there, and so did Jimmy. I walked over to her and by then she had jerked her arm back and away from Jimmy. I took her hand and she came with me to the boarding house. She sobbed and cried as I held her. She really felt pain and betrayal. I explained to her about the wrong boy that I got mixed up with in school, and told her to make good choices and not to give Jimmy a second thought, as all I wanted for her was to be happy in life, unlike me and my life that I have just come from.

"Kayla finally stopped crying as I had been wiping away each and every one of her tears. She told me that she would try very hard to take my advice. From the look on her face, I assume that this is something that she is struggling with right now and may need another talk later on.

"The secret about the mountain is bothering her. I know that she does recognize the fact that you can't tell her anything about what you and the rest of the military are doing up there. She loves you and is very proud of you, but like me when my dad left on missions that I didn't understand, there was that thought in my mind on whether he would return to me again safely. Kayla lost her mom, and is not prepared to lose you as well. When she got ready to leave here, I walked her outside and asked her if she wanted me to take her home. She told me that she would be okay, and that the walk would help her to think and clear her mind. I stood outside watching her, until I couldn't see her anymore. She also told me that she is afraid when you are gone at night, and I told her that if it is okay with you, that she is welcome here with me any time of the day or night.

"The next day, I had a visit from Jimmy himself. He knocked on my door and I thought it might be you. He placed his foot securely inside my doorway so that I couldn't shut the door. He told me to stay out of his and Kayla's business, and if I didn't, to be very afraid. I responded back, telling him that I had no fear and that I thought she would be better off with someone other than a sleaze-bag like himself. This made him even madder, but eventually he moved his foot, and as he left his words were that I should be very afraid of him as he was capable of anything and that I would pay for what I had done.

"I again saw him and the punks he hangs out with, standing against a car watching me. I walked over to them and told them that if they were trying to scare me, it wasn't working. One of the boys told Jimmy that he wasn't going to get into trouble because of him, and that if he wanted Kayla to go and talk to her. I didn't hear Jimmy's reply back to him, as I kept walking. Since then, I haven't seen or heard from any of them. But tonight, when we were walking into the restaurant, I saw a car load of boys in a car that could have been them. I felt at the time like we had been followed, to see where we went, and if Kayla was with us. Tonight might have been the time he chose to talk to her again."

Now Mark spoke. "The night when I returned home late is the same night that I believe you are referring to. Kayla was crying. I asked her what was wrong, and she just told me that she had watched a sad movie. She was probably not wanting to get me involved as she knows that I would have hunted Jimmy down. I will talk to her more about this tomorrow, when I can. She turned 18 last month, Brenda. She is at the age where I can't shut her in her room and tell Jimmy's parents to keep him away from my little girl. All I can do, like you, is to try to get through to her through words and keep telling her to make good choices.

"Jimmy had no right coming here to bother you and to try to scare you with him and his friends. I am sorry for that, and when I see him, I will make it perfectly clear to NEVER do that again to you!! As for tonight, you might be right. When I get home, if Kayla is still awake, I will ask her if Jimmy came over. If he did, I will make sure that he doesn't come over to our home again to talk to her. She is my only child and I will protect her the best way I know how to do.

"There is so much that I would like to tell you about. You are a precious lady and don't deserve to be disrespected in any way, or harassed by punks. Tomorrow night is the prom. I am hoping that you will come to the house for dinner again. I know that Kayla would love it too. She would love showing off her new dress that you were a part of helping her pick out in the store."

"I would love it too. I have to ask you this question. Is her date Jimmy?"

"No. A different boy asked her out, and she said yes, that she would go with him. I should have asked more questions when she told me that an old movie made her cry. Maybe at that moment she would have told me the story that she told you."

"If it is okay, I would like to be the cook tomorrow night," I told him. "I can stop at the grocery store on my way over to your home and get the food that I will be preparing for you. This will give Kayla more time to get ready for her date."

"That would be very nice of you, and yes, I know that Kayla would feel the same way. Any time you are ready after you get off of work, come on over. I am, as far as I know, only going to be gone in the morning. Having the evening together will give us more time to all be together."

"I can do that. I should be there by about four o'clock."

"I will see you tomorrow. Right now I think it is very late, and I don't want you to get in trouble with the boarding house owner for my being here. I also need to check on Kayla, to see if she is still awake, so I can talk to her some, to see if Jimmy and his gang of punks showed up tonight while we were out. I need to tell her that a very smart lady talked to her the other day and gave her very good advice to stay away from Jimmy, and that she needs to listen to her," Mark said with a smile.

At that time Mark walked over to me. He put my head gently between his hands and softly kissed my forehead. Then we said good night and he left. I wasn't quite sure of what he meant when he did this. Was he thanking me for being there for Kayla, or was he starting to have feelings for me? Time would tell.

It was late and I locked my door and went to bed. I was happy that we had talked. I knew now that he and the military were aware of everything that the people in Hope were saying, and I also knew that they, being the military, knew how to handle it. It would mean a good night of sleep for me and a relaxed mind from everything that I had been wanting and needing to make him aware of.

— 5 —

Trouble Waiting to Happen

The next day at work went quickly and I was prepared for once again a fun night with Kayla until she left, and then with Mark. The only unknown problem at the time with those plans was something that I didn't know about or expect was getting ready to happen. This involved my making right choices and no mistakes.

After changing my clothes and going to the grocery store to get the food that we would eat, I then drove to their home. I rang the doorbell and Kayla answered the door. She was again anxious to see me as I was her.

"Come in, Brenda. Dad told me that you are going to be the cook tonight. I can't wait to eat what you are fixing. Thank you for doing dinner. I am excited as this will be the last high school prom that I attend. I can't wait to see who the prom queen is going to be this year."

"You are welcome, and I can understand your excitement. I remember mine and I, too, was very excited to find out who the queen was as well. Unfortunately, it wasn't me." I giggled and carried the food to the kitchen.

Kayla showed me where all the pots and pans were and helped me put the food in the fridge until I was ready to cook dinner. We returned to the living room to talk. She had brought me a tall glass of iced tea, and as we were sitting there talking, Mark came down the stairs.

"Brenda, I am so glad that you came early today. I will go get a drink of tea and be right back to talk with you and Kayla."

"Okay, and I, too, am excited to be a part of Kayla's big night," I replied.

"Your dad and I had a great time last night, Kayla. I wish you could have been a part of it. I have driven around town since I got here, looking at the stores and old buildings that looked to me like they should have fallen or been torn down. I couldn't believe my eyes when I saw the nice restaurant where we ate."

"Dad took me there before. Yes, it is very nice. There are other places to go to that are just as nice," Kayla replied.

"Maybe you can show them to me someday," I suggested.

"I would love to."

Mark had returned to the living room. We sat there talking about many things. After about an hour, I told them that it was time for me to prepare our dinner.

"Brenda, thank you for talking to me the other day," said Kayla. "I talked to Dad about it also, when he returned last night. While you and Dad were gone, I had a visitor. You were right about Jimmy. He was very persistent about talking to me. He kept ringing the doorbell and pounding on the door. At first I thought maybe it was Dad and he had forgotten his wallet or key to the front door. I don't like opening the door when Dad is gone, till I ask who is there. When Jimmy said it was him and kept insisting on coming into the house so we could talk, I told him to go away as I had nothing more that I wanted to talk to him about. He was very angry and stood at the door, pounding on it. He did this for a while longer and then I heard his car start up and he drove away. I knew he was mad at me for not letting him in here, but I didn't care. I remembered what you had told me, and I wanted to make sure that I made good choices."

"Kayla, you did the right thing. You have a beautiful life waiting for you, and if you included Jimmy in it, your dreams and your life would be shattered," I responded as

I gave her a well deserved hug. What I had told her had made a difference.

I returned to the kitchen and before long the food that I prepared was being served. It was very special for me, sitting at their table, holding hands together and thanking God for the food he had provided us to eat. This meal was a thank you to both of them for all the kindness they had shown me, a city girl who came here with her heart on her sleeve, who needed real friends. This I had found in them. This extraordinary beautiful time that I spent with my new friends was not only helping them, but also helping me to live again. I knew that I could cherish and count on them as they could me for the rest of our lives.

Mark helped me clear the table and as he read the newspaper, I did the dishes and cleaned the kitchen. When I was all done, I set the rubber gloves on the counter, and then Mark and I watched Kayla, the beautiful princess, walk down the stairs. She was shining from head to toe.

Mark walked over to her and hugged and kissed her. I stood there in amazement of how that beautiful young woman had turned herself into a fairy princess in such a short time.

"Kayla, you are beautiful," I told her.

"You are gorgeous, honey," Mark said as he stood and looked at his young 18-year-old daughter, who looked like a fashion model turning around and posing for us in order to show off her new dress. A tear fell from Mark's right eye and he said, "I wish that your mom could see you now."

Kayla hugged her dad and me. She thanked us both for our compliments and also told Mark, with a tear in her eye, that she as well wished that her mom could have been there to see her, but that she wanted to believe that Annie was always watching over her from Heaven, like the day she had protected her from the tree that had fallen through the top of the roof of the car.

When I heard those words coming from Kayla, I stood there with tears streaming from my eyes. There was no doubt in my mind that I had been blessed with two of the best friends anyone could ever want or need.

The doorbell rang and we knew that Kayla's date was there to pick her up. Kayla went to answer the door. Mark and I wiped tears from our eyes as we stood there, looking at each other and feeling proud as Kayla was going to be the prettiest girl at the prom tonight.

When she answered the door, she said, "Come in, Bobby. I want you to meet my dad and my best friend, Brenda."

"I am pleased to meet both of you," Bobby said. "I promise to have her home shortly after the prom is over with."

"We are pleased to meet you as well, Bobby," Mark replied as he smiled at both of them. "Either Brenda or myself will be waiting up for Kayla's return. Have a safe trip, and Kayla, have a blast tonight. You, too, Bobby."

Bobby was tall with short, blond, curly hair, dressed in a nice light blue suit. He was very cute and wasn't wearing the punk look like Jimmy. He was polite and looked like he came from a good stable home. Even though I wasn't Kayla's mother, Annie, I knew that this was the kind of guy that she would want her daughter to be with tonight.

"Well, we watched our little angel walk out the door," Mark said.

"Yes, we did," I replied, wondering at that moment if Mark was referring to me or to his late wife whom he loved very much.

The phone rang and Mark walked over to answer it as he wiped away a tear that was falling from his left eye.

"Yes, General Cox."

There was silence, and then Mark said, "Okay, I am headed there now. I will alert every man on post to follow me up there. I will see you soon," Mark replied with somewhat of a terrorized sound to his voice.

"Is everything okay, Mark?" I asked.

"No, Brenda, things have gone from bad to worse on the mountain. Please stay here and wait for Kayla. In fact, please just stay the night. Don't let her leave when she gets home, no matter what she hears at the prom."

"Yes, I will stay here the whole night and protect her. Be careful, Mark."

"I will do the best I can," Mark answered as he walked out the door.

I sat down on the couch to wait for Kayla. It was going to seem like an eternity before she came through the door after the prom. I turned the television on for some entertainment, hoping it would somehow take my mind off what Mark had just said, pertaining to whatever it was on the mountain that had gone from bad to worse. I knew he would do his best to come home safely.

As I sat there sipping my tea, I heard, "We are interrupting all broadcasting stations to bring you an important broadcast. DO NOT TURN OFF YOUR TELEVISION!"

I sat up, hunched forward on the couch, to listen to what the broadcaster had to say.

His words continued, "We have been authorized to let everyone know in the town of Hope that NASA has notified us that there is an object that has been picked up on their radar. They are in contact with the President, to give them the go-ahead to shoot it out of the sky. You are advised that whatever this object is, and we are not being told what it is at this moment ... but we are being told that it is traveling at a high rate of speed. NASA has been tracking this object as it is approaching Earth. They have been watching it since it was about 200,000 miles past the planet Mars. You are advised to stay in your home and not go anywhere near the mountain outside of Hope, as it appears to be headed here. Do not interfere with the procedure of the military! Again, this message has been brought to you by your local television network. I will update you as more news becomes available."

I sat there, thinking what Mark would want me to do. Would he want me to continue waiting for Kayla, or go to the school and get her? Whatever decision I made, it had to be a quick one. There was no time to lose.

I heard a knock at the door, and so I jumped up off the couch to run to the front door to answer it. When I opened the door, it was Bobby, but no Kayla. He was in an extreme panic, and he said, "Brenda, Jimmy came from nowhere. He grabbed her and told her that she was coming with him. I tried to stop him, but couldn't. He told me that he didn't want to hurt either Kayla or me, but he would if he had to. I couldn't stop him as he shoved her in his car and drove away. She didn't have time to jump out. What do we do, Brenda? What do we do?" Bobby yelled out.

"Did he give a clue as to where he was taking her?" I asked.

"He said that he was going to take her to the mountain, so that they could be alone and talk. This is what I overheard him tell her."

"Okay, Bobby, I will go to the mountain and find her. I want you to go home and tell your parents what happened, and to call the police department, and for them to be on the lookout for Jimmy's car. Also tell them where Jimmy said he was taking her."

"Okay, I will do that now," Bobby replied.

"Thank you, and I am going to go get her and bring her home," I replied.

We both left the house, going in different directions. Bobby in his car, going to his house. Me in mine, going to get Kayla, and hoping that the police met me there to help.

I drove faster than usual, and as I was driving I remembered what Kayla had told me the other day and what Jimmy had said. The old road was the same road that he liked to take, which was out by where we had gone hiking and rappelling the other day. That was where Kayla had seen him out parked with Sue Ann. I was told that day that the road went up on the mountain and this was the route that I was going to take.

I turned off the highway and watched every connecting road, to see if I could find Jimmy's car. It was starting to get dark and I wanted to find Kayla, if possible, before that happened. I turned on the radio to listen, to see if there had been another update, and so far they had none. I saw many people out on the highway, and the back road driving up toward the mountain in the direction that I was going. These people were going up there to see what they had been wondering about for a while, and they would either get stopped before they could get up the mountain, or be chased away by the military. They had to have heard the report from television as I had.

I passed several people who were walking as well, and I knew that now was not the time to stop and give them a ride. I kept driving until I got to the road going up the mountain. The sign that was there, telling people to stay out, had either been torn down or driven through as it was lying on the ground. I kept driving, and off the road I saw Jimmy's car parked. I pulled up behind it and got out.

I went running toward the car, prepared to jerk him out of it, if need be. Instead, the car was empty, but on the ground I found a piece of Kayla's new dress. She had been trying to escape and Jimmy must have torn the dress hanging onto her. From there I wasn't sure which direction to go, so once again I stood there, thinking. Would Jimmy take her up on top of the mountain, where there were hundreds of military men and women posted, or would he take her on a trail leading up to it?

My guess was the trail, and so I started walking up it, in hopes of hearing Kayla scream. Then I would know exactly where she was. I found some blood on the ground and with fear in my mind, wondering what Jimmy had done to her, I kept walking faster. At last I heard a scream and ran in the direction of it. Jimmy had Kayla on the ground, and I was afraid of what he was about to do to her.

I yelled out, "JIMMY, LET GO OF HER!!"

Jimmy looked up and saw me and said, "Aren't you the nosy bitch! I warned you before that I was capable of anything, and you wouldn't listen to me. Now I don't just have one prisoner, I have two. Get on the ground now, and stay there!" he said as he was holding a gun in his hand. Apparently, if he couldn't have her all to himself, no one could. I had to think fast.

Kayla took her foot and kicked him as hard as she could between his legs. I picked up a huge rock and hit him over the top of his head. This knocked him to the ground. Kayla got up and we both started running as fast as we could up the mountain, where I knew we would be safe. Jimmy had recovered some and was staggering and trying to run after us.

Just before we got to the top, I saw a couple hundred people not in uniform, standing guard and not letting anyone move from where they were. Across from them I could see Mark and a man whom I thought might be the General, and also the President of our country looking up at the sky. The police officers that Bobby's parents had called were there and checking everyone.

I yelled out that the boy they were looking for was over here. They came running toward me and put Jimmy in handcuffs. They were going to take him to jail when a large, massive structure came down from the sky and landed slowly in the dirt on top of the mountain. It looked to me like it was made of a much more solid material than I had ever seen before.

The sound had become so loud that everyone was covering their ears, and our hair was blowing like a tornado whipping across the mountain. The people from town were trying to push their way closer, and the guards and other military men and women were holding them back, telling them not to move again.

The object that the television station was referring to was a huge round space ship with a bunch of blue lights on the bottom of the craft. I stood there, holding Kayla in my arms, and wasn't about to let her go. She had spotted Mark and wanted to go and stand next to him. I told her that she had to stay safe with me, and that her dad was well protected by all the military that were there with rifles in their arms pointed at the space craft. Everyone stood there in silence, waiting to see if anyone got off the ship.

Shortly after it touched the ground and the engine was turned off, a ramp that was a part of the ship came down to the ground.

— 6 —

Answers Revealed

As we stood there watching, we all saw more military soldiers surrounding the spacecraft, ready to shoot at any given moment.

A tall man with a shiny gray suit and a large helmet of some sort stepped out of the space craft onto the large ramp that came down slowly to the ground. When he took off his helmet, he looked human to all of us. He stood there speaking in our language.

He said, "We are not here to harm you. We come in peace. We just want you to release what belongs to us. For many light years, we have been watching you. We have been researching your country just as you have been watching us. We have a dream of your planet and ours being one someday, where we can travel back and forth without fear of each other.

"Our technology is much more advanced than yours is. Right now, if we wanted to, we could destroy you. As we have been watching you, we don't have to, as you are destroying each other. On our planet we look different than you are seeing me now as I stand here before you. We have picked up many things from your planet for years and taken them with us to test and experiment with.

"Even if you decide to destroy us now, there will be many more of us that will come here to destroy you. If that was our goal, we would have done it a long time ago. For many of your days in your time period, we have watched from above everything you have been doing to our space craft that you are holding captive. No one wants an all-out war. Walk away from our craft and the other one in your mountain, and let us leave here peacefully."

At that time, Mark walked closer to the man on the ramp and said, "How do we know that we can trust you to do this? Why did you choose the mountain to land one of your space crafts?"

"The men inside were instructed to land in there, to observe your human race, and to bring samples of your mountain back to us for observation. It won't be long before you will be landing on *our* planet, and when you do, you will find ours much more advanced than yours is. Like I said earlier, if we wanted to destroy you, we already would have done it."

Mark walked back to the General and the President. None of us would have ever guessed that we would be standing that close to the President of our great country.

"Mr. President, what do you want us to do? Do you want us to start shooting both space crafts, in hopes that no more of them come here, or do you want us to back away like he asks, in hopes that he is being honest with us and that they will leave peacefully?" Mark asked.

General Cox added, "Mr. President, we have all the weapons and ammunition we need to destroy them and the ship inside the mountain, if you make the call for us to do so."

"No, General, I will walk back out there with this Major Colonel and talk to him. If I believe more of what he says, I will give you a hand signal, telling you to release the ships and back away. We have to do this as there would be many more that would follow after them, and at that time we would have an all-out war."

"Okay, Mr. President, I will tell our men to walk away if I get the signal from you. Sir, you are our President. I hope you are making the right decision to walk out there. Anything could happen," General Cox replied with a worried look on his face.

"Yes, I want to speak to that man. Just watch for my signal. When you see it, follow through with dismissing the troops not just out here, but inside the mountain as well. To protect our country, I have to trust in what he says, as a war just wouldn't affect our country, but all of them. We all would be under an attack. If you see us walking back here before I give my signal, then you will know that he gave me no choice," the President replied.

I watched Mark and our President walk out to the space craft. I had to hold Kayla back, as she wanted to run after her dad. The fear of her losing him like she had her mother was tearing her apart.

"Kayla, your dad will be fine. I know he wants you to stay here with me. Don't be afraid as he and our President know what they are doing."

Sobbing, she said, "I can't lose him too, Brenda."

"You won't, Kayla," I said, wondering if I was telling her the truth or if we were all going to die that night.

The guards on the mountain were struggling to hold back the people from Hope who had come to see what the military was keeping secret. Now that they all knew, they wanted to rush the space craft. That would have only turned into a horrible disaster!

"Let us through!" yelled out one of the men.

"If we do, all of you are going to storm the space ship and get us all killed. Settle down, or we will arrest all of you and drag you off the mountain. Let the President handle this in a peaceful manner," the guard said.

"Yeah, but ..." said a man.

"Yeah, but what? You either stop this, or I am going to smack you up alongside your head personally!" the guard spoke.

With this, the people from town stood there quietly, watching our President continue to walk up to the invader that had, or at least looked like he had, come in peace.

As Kayla watched and continued to shake and sob with tears pouring from her eyes, Jimmy opened his mouth and said, "Kayla, stop crying. You always have me."

I spoke up and said, "Shut up, Jimmy! After what all you pulled tonight, you are facing some serious charges. In fact, you might be looking at many years in the state prison!"

Jimmy just stood there with his head down, probably hoping at that moment that we all did die that night, and not saying a word.

That was one night when his punk friends should be thankful that they weren't around him or with him as they, too, would be looking at many years behind bars as well.

When the President approached the man on the ramp, he said, "We all heard what you said earlier. I know how much more advanced that your planet is to ours. Maybe someday we will all be flying around in space together. I am the President of this great country that you are in now, and it is up to me to decide right now whether you live or die. For every action there is a reaction, and I want to make the right one.

"I am asking you right now, man to man, if you were being honest when you said you came here in peace and meant us no harm. I am ready to give the signal now for my military to walk away from your craft, and the one inside the mountain, if you give me your word that our planet and this area will stay safe as you go back to yours."

While the President spoke, every military man and woman stood there, waiting with their rifles pointed at the crafts, and were firmly in place, waiting for the word to shoot both ships at any time they were instructed to do so.

"Yes, I meant what I said. I know you are a great leader in your country. We have been watching you as well. We promise to leave peacefully as we didn't come here to harm anyone. Yes, someday we will all be flying in the sky. We have seen the advancements that you, too, have made, knowing that you have yet to see ours. On your planet, as you see me looking like a human being, and on my planet, I have been referred to as a man of my word."

"Okay, I will trust you," the President said. "Someday maybe we will meet again under different circumstances." At that moment, the President raised his hand and gave the signal that the General was waiting to see.

Holding our breaths, we all watched the General tell the military men and women to lower their rifles and walk away.

Mr. President and Mark walked slowly back to the General, and the man that looked like one of us walked back into his craft. When he was inside, the ramp that he had been standing on, that was controlled from inside, returned to its place on the outside of the ship.

We all stood in amazement, watching and waiting to see if it would start up to go back to its home, or if we would be shot down by their technology that they had on the outside and inside of their craft.

The General had given the order for the military inside the mountain to walk away and release the craft. It wasn't long and we heard the craft start up with the loud roaring noise again that hurt our ears. The craft inside the mountain started, and it felt like the mountain shook from the loud sound from both of the space ships. In a few minutes, the space craft inside the huge mountain flew straight up and out of the topless area.

When the one sitting outside saw that their craft that had been held captive out of fear from the military thinking everyone was in danger, saw their space ship return to the sky, it too slowly started flying upward. Again, the dust was flying from the ground and our hair was standing straight up. It was all any of us could do to stand without falling over. At last it was far enough upward that it, too, flew away in the same direction as the other one.

Everyone could finally let the air out of their lungs

and breathe. That had been a night that no one in the town of Hope, or the military men and women who were stationed there, would ever forget. Everyone had finally seen the secret hidden by the military and government. One that none of us would have ever guessed what it would be. Also, we were very close to the President of our United States of America, and had gotten to see him give a signal because he chose to trust the Alien that looked human. It was man to man, and at this moment is when they should have had the National Anthem playing. We were very proud to be Americans of our great country.

Mark saw us in the crowd and came running over to us. He could see Jimmy and the police officers hanging onto him. "Are you all right, Kayla?" he asked.

"Yes, Dad. I am fine now that you are here," Kayla replied as she hugged him.

"What happened, Brenda?"

"It's a long story, Mark. To make it short, Jimmy forced Kayla into his car in front of the school, and Bobby came to tell me about it. He brought her here to the mountain with a gun," I explained.

"Officer, I will be down to the police station to press charges," said Mark. "I want him locked up."

"We are ready to take a statement from your daughter, and anyone else who has one to give us when all of you arrive there," an officer commented.

Jimmy was 19 and would be tried as an adult. I hoped Kayla didn't need counseling for what she had experienced.

Our President had just left on a helicopter to return to Washington, D.C. The military men and women had been dismissed, Mark and Kayla took me back to my car, and I went to pick up Bobby and take him with me to give our statements of what we had seen and heard from Jimmy.

There at the police station, we met Mark and Kayla, who were also giving them the information that they needed.

All of us wanted Jimmy to be locked up for a long time. From there, Mark, Kayla and I went to their home, where I was asked to spend the night.

In the morning, my being an early riser, I was the first one out of bed. Because of the eventful night on the mountain, the owner of the café, where I worked, decided for that day to keep the café closed. There would be no work for me until tomorrow.

As I sat drinking coffee that I had fixed, Mark and Kayla came down the stairs. They both were wearing a big smile, unlike how I had pictured in my mind what they would be wearing.

"Good morning, Brenda," Mark said.

"Good morning to both of you."

"Did you sleep well?" Kayla asked.

"Yes, I did, and better than I have in a long time," I replied.

Mark and Kayla continued to smile and I said, "I'm happy to see that both of you are okay after last night's events."

"We are fine. Dad and I talked before we went to bed, and again this morning before we came downstairs. There is something that Dad wants to talk to you about, and just so you know, I am very happy about it," Kayla said as she hugged me.

"Okay," I said, wondering what Mark and I would discuss as I hugged her back.

Kayla walked back up the stairs to return to her room, and Mark came over to sit beside me. He was still smiling and my curiosity of what he was about to say was out of control.

"Brenda, I want to thank you again for being there for Kayla last night, and all the other times she needed help. You are a godsend to us. When Annie was killed, I felt like my world had crumbled before me. I had a six-year-old daughter that was depending on me to not only be Dad, but also to play the role of Mom as well. I had a nanny come in to live with us as Kayla was growing up. I couldn't take her with me everywhere I went. After she reached a certain age, it was time to let the nanny go. Kayla wasn't a little girl any longer. She had learned how to cook, clean and be responsible, as well as resourceful. She was a young woman and looking more and more like Annie every day.

"I had forgotten how much she needed a woman in her life until you came to Hope. You are not just a great friend to both of us, but an important part of our lives. After everything you have seen and been put through, we aren't sure if you plan on staying here. If you are, we want you to move out of the boarding house and in here with us. To us, you are family now," said Mark.

This was not the conversation I had expected, but one that made me smile as well. Kayla and Mark meant the world to me, and had made my life complete. What I had experienced here was a piece of cake compared to the way it had been before I had come to the town of Hope. They had given me so much hope for a happier future.

I knew that in the bank I had enough money to buy anything and everything anyone would possibly want from the settlement of my divorce. Even my ex-husband couldn't keep me from having what I had earned, no matter what he had said in the courtroom.

I looked into Mark's gorgeous blue eyes and said, "Yes, Mark, I would love to live here with you and Kayla. I really didn't know what a real family was like until I met you and Kayla. You both are very important to me."

Kayla, who had just come downstairs, had heard just enough of our talk to know that I would be moving in with them. She was very pleased and came over to hug me and tell me that she was so excited about my being there full time.

Mark hugged me as well, and this time, instead of kissing me on the forehead, he gave me a kiss on the lips.

The school had rescheduled the prom, and it was

another trip to the clothing shop to pick out a new dress for Kayla. Bobby and Kayla had a great time at the prom as Jimmy sat at the county jail, awaiting his arraignment. His punk friends got scared and left town.

Even with all the money I had in the bank, I continued to work at the small café. I had gotten to know many of the townspeople and loved my job.

The people in town looked happy again, and the talk of storming the mountain was a thing of the past as everyone once again was allowed back on it.

Mark and I became closer and more than friends. I still feel as if Kayla played a big part in the talk Mark and I had that morning. She was playing matchmaker and it worked, as Mark and I had fallen in love. I knew I could never take away the love that he still had in his heart for Annie, and I didn't ever want to.

All three of us had a new beginning and a long life together being a family.

The morning that Mark and I said our vows to each other at the same mountain that held a lot of people, Kayla stood next to me as my maid of honor. She would always be not just my new daughter, but my best friend.

Once again, the entire military men and women from the Army post and the townspeople cheered when the ceremony was over. I turned my back to them and threw my bouquet.

Kayla had backed up, and as it went flying through the air, she jumped up to catch it. Standing next to her was Bobby. Mark and I looked at each other and smiled as Kayla looked at Bobby and smiled. Someday, years from now maybe, there would be another wedding to attend. The only difference being Mark and I would be the proud parents of the beautiful bride that would be standing before us.

The unknown road going nowhere that I thought I would continue on turned out to be a road that led me to a life that I had dreamed about for many years of happiness with Mark, Kayla, and eventually our son Kyle and our other daughter, Karla.

PART 2

SHADOWS IN THE NIGHT

— 1 —

Loneliness and Despair

A young man dressed in a pair of jeans and a shirt that had been washed many times was lying, destitute, on a park bench in Los Angeles, California, waiting for the sun to rise. He lay inside an old sleeping bag given to him by his deceased grandfather, who served our country in World War II.

Like every day, he walked up and down many side-walks, looking for work. He hid his sleeping bag and back-pack full of dirty clothes that he washed with hand soap in empty bathrooms at convenience stores. At night, while he slept, his clothes that he had placed on a nearby bench dried.

For weeks and months, he had been eating out of garbage dumpsters the food that paying customers had thrown away.

His wife of many years had left him in the night with a note that read: "I can't do this when you wake up, but for now I need to take Sarah to my sister's house. There we will be safe until you can find work. Take care of yourself. Sarah and I will wait for you to call. We can't sleep on a park bench any longer."

Sarah was his five-year-old daughter. The young man knew that the reason why she'd left in the night from the park bench that she shared with Sarah every night was something that she had to do. It would have been harder for all of them in the morning, and she was right by doing this. He was heartbroken and penniless.

Before long his mind became weak and strained. Many nights passed, and before he would drift off to sleep, he would see shadows of what he wanted to believe were those of his grandfather, who had raised him. There were times as well when he yearned to see and be with his wife and daughter so much that he believed the shadows were from them coming back to visit him.

He was extremely tired from lack of sleep, and lonely, feeling despair. He wondered if he was maybe losing his mind, or if the shadows were there to protect him from others who could hurt or kill him as he slept on the bench. Sometimes he believed that they were shadows of himself before his life had changed.

This young man I am speaking about is me, John Dubois. I am only 25 years old. Because of my living conditions every night for months, trying to stay warm and feeling like a man in his 50s or 60s, my bones ache from the cold, and my back hurts from miles of walking each day, trying to find someone who will give me the chance that I need to better myself again. I want my family to come back to me. I want to support them the way that I once did. That is when my loneliness and feelings of being worthless will go away. In spite of everyone who passes me on the street, thinking that I am nothing but a bum looking for a handout, I always worked hard at my previous job.

When the company I worked for closed their doors to everyone who had worked for them and shut down their business, it sent everyone out onto the street. We prayed that we all could find work again, and that the next day would bring us a new start that we needed.

I am resourceful and won't give up. Each day I push myself harder than the day before. Someday I will feel productive again, with a sense of pride.

The night our home caught on fire, our daughter Sarah had gone to the kitchen to get a drink. At the time, she was only three-and-a-half, and with her wanting to believe that she was a big girl, she scooted a stool over to the sink. My wife Bonnie and I stood at the front door, waiting on her, as we believed she had gone to her room to get her doll. We had no idea what she was doing, and that when she scooted the stool over, she accidentally bumped the knob on the gas stove and lit it.

After she was finished, she scooted the stool back, not knowing that she had also, in the process, moved a dish towel to the flame on the stove. That night we were on our way to a neighbor's home for dinner and conversation. Bonnie had the window by the stove open as it was a warm night. We had no idea that the wind was about to blow a flame close to the dish towel, just enough to catch it on fire.

When Sarah joined us in the living room, we all walked out of our home for the last time. Walking down the sidewalk, we smelled smoke and then heard a large explosion. When we turned around to see what it was and where it came from, we could see that our home was burning down.

Our neighbor called 9-1-1, and by the time the fire department got there, everything was mostly destroyed. Even our car, which had been parked in our garage. The sad part was that we had just paid off our home and had cancelled our homeowner's fire protection policy. So we were not insured any longer. We had planned on getting it renewed after we had our car paid off. Now we not only had no home, but also no car.

The insurance company determined that the car was destroyed from a fire within our home and wanted the homeowner's insurance company to pay for it. I had to explain to them that I had no insurance at that time, and so I was told that they wouldn't pay me for my car.

There were many phone calls back and forth, arguing

with them, and then finally we decided that we weren't going to win the fight, so we gave up, which left us not only homeless, but also without a vehicle to drive, and not enough money in the bank to buy another one.

So there we were with very little that hadn't been destroyed from the fire, living with Bonnie's parents until my unemployment came through for me.

At that time I continued to look for a job day after day, in hopes of finding something before my unemployment ran out. With so many people being out of work at that time, the job market was not good. After a year of staying with my in-laws, we decided that we had stayed long enough and bought a bus ticket to California.

We had some money left over for food and for a cheap room, where all three of us slept each night, and then our last dime was gone. I was convinced that it would only take a few days in a big city and I would have a job. We thought that we would be all right sleeping on a park bench each night and walking the streets during the day with Sarah.

It was hard on Bonnie and Sarah. They continued to stay with me until they couldn't do it any longer, knowing that I eventually would get a job and then we could be a family again. That is when she left.

Today is different than the other ones. I am going to a different part of the city. I had passed by there on my way to a company where I had applied a few days ago. This one was a huge transporting company that employed workers to load and arrange large boxes to ship to different parts of the world.

I, for the first time in a long while, was having good thoughts about this and needed the job. It wasn't the type of work that I had done before, but it was something I knew I could do.

When I arrived there, I saw a man standing guard next to a big flatbed truck. He was wearing a uniform, so I knew he was the company's security guard.

"Hello, can you tell me where the office is?" I asked, feeling somewhat nervous. I was afraid of denial and insecurity again when I did get to talk to someone in the office.

"Yes, go in this door and you will see off to the right some stairs. It's quite a climb as the office is on the third floor. When you have gotten to the third floor, you will make a right and follow the hall all the way down until you come to another hall, where you go right or left. Take a left turn and keep going until you come to the fourth room on the right side. That is the office," the guard explained.

"Okay. Thank you for the directions."

When I entered the building, I saw several workers. Some were taking boxes off conveyor belts and loading them onto dollies. Others were sorting boxes and arranging them on shelves as they stood on a tall ladder.

I wasn't sure what the company shipped out on big trucks and barges, but I did know I was willing to do any manual labor that they asked of me, to be able to get my family back with me and start living again with shelter and food.

As I climbed the stairs, wondering why there was no elevator, there was a man who looked mad coming down the stairs in my direction. He stopped and turned around, yelling up the stairs, "You won't get by with doing this to me! I am not the one you are looking for!"

The man then turned and started walking downward again, fast, and grumbling to himself as he walked past me. I wasn't sure what he was referring to, but from the angry look on his face, it would be pointless of me to tell him to have a nice day.

I kept walking and came to my first hall. With each step, I became more anxious and wondering why that man on the stairs yelled out the words he had said.

When I arrived at the office and had entered the room, there was a small-built woman wearing black-framed glasses, with brown hair pulled back, sitting behind her desk. She saw me standing at the door and said, "Can I help you with something?"

"Yes, you can. I would like to apply for a job," I replied as my legs shook some and my knees were knocking together.

"Okay. Please have a seat and I will get you an application." She got up from her desk and walked to a file cabinet, then pulled out a large drawer to get one for me to fill out. When she found one, she brought it to me, smiling. Then she returned to her desk. I could see that she was very efficient at her job.

As I looked down at the application, I saw that at the top was the name of the company, "Barnes Transporting." I had heard about this business years ago from my grandfather, and didn't ever believe that my life would bring me here.

I continued answering questions on each one of the pages. When I looked at the one that asked me for my contact information, I sat staring at the question, pondering what I should say. Did I tell them that I was living on a park bench, or make up a fake address? The only choice I had was to be honest with them and hope for a good response back.

After I completed the application, I walked over to the lady at her desk and handed the application back to her. She looked down at it briefly, reviewing all the answers to make sure that I had answered them all. Then she asked me to sit back down and she would take it to Mr. Barnes, who might want to interview me.

I sat down, leaning forward in my chair, looking at the floor as if I, at any moment, could jump up and run out of the room. If he did interview me, it would be the first one I'd had since Bonnie, Sarah and I had come to Los Angeles.

After a while, the lady came out of the room she had gone into and told me that Mr. Barnes would like to speak to me.

I looked up and smiled at her. This was the most hope that I'd had so far.

I followed her into a big office, where a short, stocky bald, elderly man sat. When I entered his room, he looked up from my application that he held in his hands. His glasses slid part way down on his nose and he was looking over them at me.

"Please sit down, Mr. Dubois. I see that you have quite a work history for as young as you are. I knew Bob Weatherton personally as I grew up in Atlanta, where you were employed. It's a shame that Bob had to let his company that he built from the ground up go like he did. I know this hurt him as much as it did all of you.

"I also am curious about your last name. I was in the Army. I served in the war with a man by the name of Ralph Dubois. Are you related to or know this man? He would probably be about my age," Mr. Barnes said.

"My grandfather's name was Ralph. He also lived in Atlanta after the war. Unfortunately, he got sick a few years ago from pneumonia and passed away at St. Rose Hospital."

I continued, "The layoff came at a bad time of the year for all of us, but we did understand why Mr. Weatherton had to do what he did. The economy had spiraled downward and no one wanted to hire after that. This is how my wife Bonnie, my daughter Sarah and I ended up here.

"Bonnie and Sarah stayed with me for several months, but left for now, in hopes of being able to come back soon after my living conditions change. I am sure you saw from my application that I am homeless," I added, feeling more comfortable than I had felt since I entered the building.

"Yes, I did notice. When I saw this, it took me back in time to when I was 19 years old," said Mr. Barnes. "My father and I struggled to have a normal relationship. While I was growing up, he expected more out of me than

I could do or give to him. I found myself out living on the streets after high school. The war had started and no one was hiring, and several of the businesses had closed their doors.

"I, like you, was cold, afraid and hungry. I walked the streets, looking for work. After many months of this, I had a draft notice waiting for me, telling me that I had a date with Uncle Sam, and now was an enlisted man serving in the Army. Then I was on my way to Europe.

"Since then, I became successful and have opened not just my door at home to people, but also have employed many homeless people. I never forgot where I came from. Now I am hiring you, John. I will give you the chance you need to find your way back to society again."

At that moment I felt at peace for the first time in months. I was forever grateful. "Thank you, Mr. Barnes," I said as I shook his hand.

"You can start tomorrow morning. I am putting you on the loading dock. It's back-breaking work, but I am sure you can handle it as you are young and strong," Mr. Barnes said as he smiled at me.

"I can do this and I won't let you down," I replied, smiling back at him. I again thanked him and walked out of his room. I then told the lady at the desk that I had gotten the job, and she told me to return to her in the morning and she would show me where to go each day.

I told her that I would be there waiting for her, very early.

— 2 —

Suspicions

That night, after many months, I finally felt like I had hope. As I curled up in my grandfather's sleeping bag, I knew that before long I would have a warm place to sleep. The shadows that seemed to surround me would no longer have to be there to protect me from the dangers of the city.

The next morning, when I entered the office, the lady behind the desk walked with me to a different part of the building. "Mr. Dubois, we are a big company that transports large and small items for many companies. They depend on us to handle and move every box carefully, but quickly. I don't know if Mr. Barnes told you this. For the past month, we have had someone stealing from us. The security guards have tried to catch the person or persons doing it. Even with all of them watching, it isn't enough."

"Mr. Barnes didn't tell me any of this, but with me knowing now what is happening here, I will watch as well. I am very grateful for the opportunity to be working here, and will help any way that I can," I told her, meaning every word that came out of my mouth.

"Thank you, Mr. Dubois."

"Please call me John," I said.

"Okay, John. My name is Alice."

Alice introduced me to the foreman who was waiting for us. He was tall, heavy, and when he spoke out, everyone paid attention to what he said.

"Mr. Dubois, we are pleased to have you working

here. Alex Norton is my name," he said as he shook my hand firmly.

"Thank you. I am grateful for this job. You will see that I am a hard worker," I replied.

Alex took me around to familiarize me with each step that happens before anything came to the loading dock to be loaded out for shipment. I learned a lot from him that day and was working side by side with the other workers, who appeared to me to be good at their job. The entire process was running smoothly.

At the end of the day, we punched out from the time clock and walked through a gate that took us on the other side of the large building and work area. This was where the workers parked their cars, just as I would when I could afford another one.

That night as I laid down to sleep, I was thinking about what Alice had told me. The stealing was more than likely coming from someone who knew the operation of where everything was kept inside the fence, and they knew of an easy way into the working area without being spotted by the security guards. My guess was that this was taking place at night instead of during the day.

Tomorrow, when I could, I would be looking around at not just the other workers, but the layout of the area. After a few days of observation, if I didn't see anything out of the ordinary, I would spend a night in the bushes to see if I was right, that all of this was happening when everyone was home and asleep.

The next day as I worked, I listened to conversations and watched everyone. About midway through the day, I glanced in the direction of two men who were talking to one of the security guards. None of them saw me looking at them.

It was time for me to walk closer to where they were standing, in hopes of hearing them. Until this mystery was solved, I couldn't trust anyone, and with my determination to help Mr. Barnes, I wouldn't give up until the crook, or crooks, were caught. As I moved closer to the three men, I heard the security guard talking.

"You are getting careless, Matt. Do you have any idea what this would cost us?"

"I am not the only one that is making mistakes, Jim. There is something in there that could take care of us for the rest of our lives," Matt replied as he stood there with his hands in his pockets.

"We will make this happen, Jim. Just be patient as this could take some time," said a man whom they referred to as Big O. By the size of the guy, I could see why they called him that. He looked like he could pick up a box that weighed 500 pounds by himself.

When I moved a little closer to them, they stopped talking, and Matt and Big O went back to work. The security guard wandered off in a different direction. I realized that the words they had spoken wasn't enough information for me to assume that they were the ones involved.

I kept working and watching everyone. There was an opportunity to check out the fence that surrounded the company. The foreman sent me and three other men to the gate to unload a big truck that had delivered more boxes that would need to be loaded at the dock.

As I walked the fence line, everything looked secure. The fence was sturdy and strong. The only way inside the company yard, once the gate was locked, was to climb over the huge fence. This would take a tall person who was big, to be able to lift that much weight by himself. This is when Big O crossed my mind as he was not only very tall, but also had the arms of a body builder.

My direction again focused on Jim, Matt and Big O. Each day I would continue to listen to their conversations and those of others as well, since I could be wrong about the three men.

When it was the end of my shift, I stood outside the fence once more, watching to see if maybe I could observe something that might give me more of an insight on what was going on.

After a half an hour of standing close to the bushes, I saw Matt and Big O come out of the gate. They should have left the grounds when the rest of us did. While they walked and talked, I could see that they were looking at me. Neither one of them was smiling.

As they approached the spot where I was standing, Matt had a question for me. "Why are you still here?"

I had to come up with something fast and gave them the only answer that came to my mind. "My car broke down on me this morning, and I'm waiting for a friend that should be here soon to pick me up and take me home."

"Okay," Matt said as they walked away, looking at me with tough eyes, like I had better not be lying. I had given them the right answer, and yes, I was lying.

Once again, as I tried to sleep that night, I thought about many things. My wife and daughter were safe, warm and not struggling, and my life could be in danger if I continued to try to solve the mystery of who was stealing from Mr. Barnes. Knowing this, I had to continue as he was giving me a chance to pull myself out of the gutter, where my life had taken me. The shadows in the night were still there and would continue to be there until I was out of there.

In the morning at the loading dock, I kept my eyes focused on not just the boxes that we were loading onto a big truck that was going to take them to a large barge where they would be shipped out, but also on Matt and Big O. Occasionally I would get a glimpse of Jim, the security guard, walking around the area and focusing his eyes on me. My thoughts were that he had realized that I was a little too curious when I moved closer to him and his two friends yesterday, and he didn't like it. Was I a target now?

During the afternoon, when it was our break time, I sat down on the ground like the other workers did. I saw Matt and Big O coming from a part of the building that was off limits to any of the workers, unless we were instructed to enter. This part of the building was where they kept their more expensive items, like diamond jewelry, crystal, paintings and anything else of value. The only ones who had a key to the door were Mr. Barnes and the security guards. This is where Jim would be involved. There was something in there of extreme value, and it appeared to me as if they wanted it.

Jim continued to watch me as I continued to work my shift. I was sure now that this mystery was an inside theft and that Matt, Big O and Jim had made me very suspicious of all three of them.

When the workers left to go home, I continued to stand outside the fence line. I hadn't seen Matt or Big O come out of the gate, and I was sure they were still in there, talking to Jim.

Today, if I was asked why I was still there, I would need to use my car as an excuse again.

Within the hour, I saw them rounding the corner of the building. They had noticed me as well and were talking as they walked toward me. As they approached, I could see from their expressions that they weren't happy to see me there.

"Why are you here again tonight?" Matt asked with an unfriendly tone to his voice.

"Oh, my car is in the shop, getting worked on, and I am waiting for my ride to show up," I replied, smiling at them. Being suspected, as I knew I was, I had to look friendly and stay calm.

"That excuse works for today, but not much longer," said Big O. "Another thing you better remember is that we don't like nosy people. Watch what you're doing, so you don't get hurt!" He looked down at me with a serious look on his face as the three of them walked away.

That excuse had run its course and I could see that they didn't believe my story. Now, instead of just watching their back to see what they were doing, I had to watch my own, to protect myself.

It was time to go to Mr. Barnes and let him know what I had heard and witnessed. Maybe I hadn't given it enough time, but I was one man up against three. I had no weapon to protect myself and no desire to get hurt or killed.

Because of the time and the fact that Mr. Barnes had probably left for the day, I would go to the office first thing in the morning and speak to either him or Alice about this.

I didn't see the car leave the parking area like the night before and was wondering if they were staying there long enough to see if I was telling them the truth, and also to see where I lived. Because of this lie, things were becoming complicated, and I wasn't sure what to do. If I started walking, they would think that I had either seen the person who was picking me up, or they would follow me to see where I went.

My gut feeling told me to stay put as they would only wait there so long, and then they would leave. After a half an hour of waiting, I was right as they did leave.

I knew what my plan was for tomorrow, and after they were out of sight, I took a different route "home" to my park bench. This time I got lucky, but I knew that it might not last much longer.

— 3 —

The Truth Unfolds

That night was much the same as I had before—with thoughts of my family and the three men, whom I was convinced were the ones who were stealing from Mr. Barnes. I lay on the park bench, trying to sleep. Then I saw a big shadow that I hadn't seen before. Not knowing what this was, I covered my head. For all I knew, it could have been Big O watching me. After a while, I went to sleep, dreaming of people that I missed.

In the morning, the first stop at the company was in Mr. Barnes' office. I needed to talk to him and wanted to do it before anyone saw me, or when I was scheduled to be at my job on the loading dock.

Alice was sitting at her desk, typing, when I opened the door.

"Good morning, Alice. Is Mr. Barnes in his office? If so, could I please talk to him?" I asked as I walked to her desk.

"No, John, he isn't planning on coming in today. He has other business that he needs to take care of. Can I help you?" she asked with a smile.

Not knowing whether I should involve her in the news that I had, I hesitated for a few seconds. Alice could see that whatever it was that I wanted to talk to Mr. Barnes about was important, so she let me know that she was Mr. Barnes' right hand, and that she had the authority to take care of anything that concerned him. Her saying this made me feel more comfortable about talking to her about the three men.

"Alice, the reason why I came here today was to discuss with Mr. Barnes about what you told me was happening here with someone stealing from the company. Because of Mr. Barnes' kindness in giving me a chance at my job on the loading dock, I made it my mission to try to help find out who is doing this."

"Go on," she urged.

"The first day, I spotted two of the workers talking to a security guard. Their demeanor was strange and they kept looking around as if to make sure no one could hear what they were talking about. Because they were talking very low, I moved closer to them in hopes of hearing what they had to say.

"When I did, I heard the security guard tell them that they were getting careless, and he asked if they knew what it would cost them. The second man told him that he was not the only one making mistakes and that there was something in there that could take care of them for the rest of their lives. The third man told the security guard that they would make it happen, and to just be patient as it could take some time.

"I didn't want to assume that they were the ones doing this, so I gave them the benefit of the doubt. As I gave it more thought, I realized that this had to be happening from someone, perhaps others that worked there and knew where everything was at. The next day I continued to watch everyone again and especially the three men. That night after work, I stood outside the gate to see if anyone came walking out with something that belonged to the company.

"The two men who were talking to the security guard came out later, after everyone had left. I had to come up with a phony excuse why I was there, so I told them that my car broke down and I was waiting for a ride. That seemed to pacify them and they walked away.

"The next day, I continued to watch them. The security guard continued to watch me. He acted skittish and like he was wondering why I was watching them. During break time, we all sat down to rest and I noticed the two men coming from the part of the building where the expensive items are kept for shipping. I know that the only ones who have a key to this place are Mr. Barnes and the security guards. I tried not to let them see that I had seen where they came from, and now I am convinced that these three men could very well be the ones you are looking for.

"Last night I stood outside the gate again, watching, and two of the men came around the corner of the building sometime after we had all got off work. Once again, I could see them looking at me and talking as they walked. They asked me the same question about why I was there, and I told them that my car was in the shop and I was waiting for my ride.

"I was told that excuse wouldn't fly again, and that if I didn't stop being nosy—as they didn't like it—that I could get hurt. I didn't know what to do as they continued to sit in the car and watch me, waiting for me to leave. After about a half an hour, they left. I took a different route walking home, hoping not to be seen, as my 'home' is the park bench.

"This is when I decided that I needed to talk to Mr. Barnes. I hate to point a finger at anyone unless I have good cause to do so, but everything is pointing in their direction, and I felt like I needed to make him aware of it," I said, feeling relieved that I had gotten to talk to someone about this.

"Wow, John. You made fast work of this," said Alice. "From what you have told me, it sounds like you might have found out who is stealing around here. Who are the men that you have been referring to?" she asked.

"The security guard's name is Jim, and the other two men are called Matt and Big O."

"Okay. I can see why you would suspect all three of them. About two months ago, we had a security guard quit as he got a better job. Mr. Barnes did his hiring from an agency downtown that has security guards. Jim is an odd one, I agree. I am not sure that when Mr. Barnes hired him, he was very impressed with his performance and capability. As for the man named Matt, I know which one you are talking about, and he has gotten into trouble here before and was given a second chance. He likes to start a fight at the loading dock and was told that if it happened again, he would be losing his job.

"Big O is the large guy that can pick up the back of a car, if need be. Mr. Barnes has kept him here because of his strong ability to move boxes that would take three men to move. He hangs around with Matt all the time. You could very well know what you are talking about, John. I am happy that Mr. Barnes hired you. You are a good worker and a nice man. When I know that Mr. Barnes is home, I will call him and relay to him what you told me."

Then she told me, "Today, don't watch them. And after work, leave right away. You can't afford to get hurt … or worse." Then Alice thanked me again for the information.

When I arrived at the loading dock, Jim, the security guard, had watched me walk from the door going upstairs to the office. He gave me a strange look and then walked away. That day I did exactly what Alice had told me and avoided Jim, Matt and Big O every chance I had.

One more time, I saw the three of them talking around the dock and I stayed away, wondering what they were talking about.

"Jim, I am like Matt, I don't trust him. We have caught him waiting outside the gate after work, making up some kind of an excuse as to why he was still there. I had Matt drop me off last night and I followed him. He lives on a bench in the park downtown. When it was darker, I stood behind a tree, watching him for a while, until he covered his head to sleep. He is homeless and I don't think anyone will miss him if we go after him tonight. We can hide him in the building where we are working to get what we want, and no one will find him for a few days. By then, depending on him, he will be alive and it won't matter how much he sings to the cops," Big O said, looking at Jim with a serious look.

"If you think that is what you need to do, then do it. I will have the door unlocked at 11:00 tonight and will be waiting for you inside the building. Just make sure that no one sees you taking him or bringing him in here. I will make sure the back gate on the side of the building is unlocked. Don't screw this up!" Jim said just before he walked away from them.

If I would have known what they had said, I would have run like the wind. Instead, I just kept working, and at the end of the day I walked out the gate before Matt or Big O saw me. I went back to the park, hoping that Alice was able to get hold of Mr. Barnes.

About 9:00 I laid down on the bench again to sleep. The big shadow wasn't there, but the other ones seemed to surround me. I felt like I wasn't alone. After I was fast asleep, I felt someone picking me up off the bench, and then someone putting tape across my mouth. I was wrapped up inside of the sleeping bag and couldn't get out, even when I struggled.

At that moment, I heard Big O telling me that it wouldn't do me any good to keep fighting him, as he was stronger than a horse. They put me in the back seat of the truck with my zipper tied on the sleeping bag with a rope to where I couldn't escape. My luck had run out and I kept wondering if this was the end for me.

When I heard the truck stop, I knew that we had reached the place where they were either going to dump me in the ocean or tie me to a tree somewhere. Instead, I saw that we had gone back to the company and were entering the same door that Matt and Big O came out of the other day. I was right, there was something in there that they wanted, and tonight was when they were going to get it.

Big O dropped me on the floor and told me that if I was a good boy, they might spare my life. I was terrified and was still wondering if Alice had talked to Mr. Barnes, and if he believed me.

Matt and Big O took boxes down and placed them on the floor. Whatever was in them must be something that would give them enough money to last a lifetime.

Jim came over to me and told me that I was just a little smarter than he thought I was and should have minded my own business. There was a part of me at that moment that wished I had. With the tape securely placed over my mouth, I couldn't say anything.

The three men continued to get everything they wanted loaded in the truck, and then they came in for one more box. They were done and I thought I was done for as well.

"What do you want me to do with him?" Big O asked Jim.

"If you shoot him, you are going to draw attention to us. There is another guard here that is patrolling the inside of the building. We need to just leave him tied up, and then leave here as quick as we can before we get spotted," Jim replied.

"I can give him one last kick for not minding his business," Matt said.

"Stop wasting our time, Matt. We are done and ready to leave," Jim commented.

The three men walked out the door and I was sure that they had gotten away with millions of dollars of whatever was kept in that room.

All of a sudden, I heard police cars pulling into the side area of the building, and I heard a security guard talking outside. Could it be possible that Jim, Matt and Big O had been caught? It wasn't long and the door opened. Standing there was Mr. Barnes. *He had believed me.*

"John, are you all right?" Mr. Barnes asked as he

removed the tape from my mouth and untied the rope that was wrapped around my sleeping bag.

"I am fine now," I said and smiled at him.

"Alice called me. John, I had wondered myself about these men for some time now. I couldn't confide in anyone but Alice, as Jim, Matt and Big O have been there for a while, and I knew they had other friends from the loading dock. I didn't know who I could trust. When I hired you, I wanted Alice to tell you about this so that you would be aware of what has been going on around here. I have tried several times to catch them in an act of stealing from me, and couldn't. They managed to do this during the day, when the other workers were busy, and no one would be the wiser. I couldn't accuse them without solid evidence. At first they stole little things and I knew it wouldn't be long and they would get greedy and the larger items would come up missing. They wanted the expensive ones.

"Tonight, I drove past here to check things out myself. When I saw a truck parked close to the entrance of this building, I knew something was happening, so I called the police. The other security guard, placed here to keep watch, is always inside the main part of the building at this time, checking each room, and Jim knew this. The boxes that they were taking were scheduled to be loaded on the barge on Monday. If they weren't caught tonight, they would have gotten away with a 300-pound gold bell, lots of diamonds and a crystal vase that is worth millions of dollars. Your insight, John, saved my company. There could have been a horrible lawsuit that would have resulted.

"Thank you, John. I knew when I hired you that you would be a huge asset to the company, and to me," Mr. Barnes said as he shook my hand.

"I'm happy I could help you," I told him. "You saved mine and my family's life when you gave me the chance that I needed with my job." I felt happy that this mystery was over with and that I wasn't shot in the process. In fact, the blood drained back into my face. I was safe.

That night Mr. Barnes took me to a motel, to a warm bed that I could sleep in for the weekend. Afterwards, he was busy at the police department, filling out paper work and making sure that Jim, Matt and Big O were sent to prison for a long time.

The next morning I walked back to the park to get my backpack, so no one would steal it. Other than my wife Bonnie and my daughter, Sarah, the sleeping bag and backpack were all that I had.

On Monday morning when I returned to work, I hid my backpack in the bushes outside the gate. Mr. Barnes told the foreman to have me come to the office. At the dock I had been greeted and cheered by my co-workers, who had already heard the news from Mr. Barnes.

When I arrived at the office, Alice gave me a big hug and told me that I had done good and thanked me for saving the company. I thanked her for trusting and believing me when I had talked to her last.

Mr. Barnes was waiting for me in his office. When I walked in, he stood up from his desk, walked over to me and also gave me a hug. "John, you have saved my company millions of dollars. I am forever grateful to you. I not only am giving you your first week of work's paycheck, but also I want to give you this."

At that moment, he handed me a set of keys to a nice home that turned out to be in a good neighborhood of the city, and a set of keys to a nice car. I was no longer homeless.

I was so overwhelmed with joy that I stood in front of Mr. Barnes and Alice with tears streaming down my face. I couldn't thank them enough. His generosity was more than I felt like I deserved.

When I walked back to the loading dock, there was another round of cheers from the co-workers waiting for me. If I wouldn't have solved the mystery of the stealing thieves, Mr. Barnes would have had to lay off everyone and sell his company in order to cover the items that would have been stolen. His insurance company would not have covered the bell, the diamonds or the crystal as it was too large of a risk for them.

After I completed my shift, Mr. Barnes took me to my new home and new car. I again told him that I was extremely grateful.

If nothing else in my lifetime so far, I had learned that no matter where a person's life takes them, there can be a silver lining waiting for them in the future. The key to it all is to keep going and not to give up. Also, to be aware of surroundings all the time, as it can change anyone's life for the good or the bad. For every action there is a reaction.

After Mr. Barnes left, I took my car to a gas station, where I hadn't gone for many months, to put gas in it. Also, I wanted to call the number on the note where my daughter, Sarah, and my wife Bonnie had been living for several months.

When I heard Bonnie's voice and gave her the good news that we could finally be together as a family again, I cried like a baby. Of course she asked me many questions, and I told her that I would explain everything when I saw her. I was sending her money to fly into LAX on Saturday.

I couldn't wait for Saturday to get here. My week at work seemed to take forever.

Then on Saturday morning, I drove to the airport to pick up my family and couldn't stop smiling the whole way there. After the plane landed and people were walking off of it, my daughter Sarah came running toward me. I embraced her and couldn't kiss her enough.

When I stood up and saw Bonnie, she was holding a surprise that I didn't know about ... or expect. It was my new baby son, Kaylob. This, Bonnie said, was the main reason why she had to leave that night. I hugged her and kissed her with more tears streaming down my face. She then placed Kaylob in my arms.

Within months, I was promoted to assistant foreman and our lives became even better than they had been in the past, all because I followed my heart wanting to help Mr. Barnes, and went with a hunch.

At night, when I am walking around, I still see shadows in the night. Before, they were shadows of who I believe were Angels watching over me at the time as I slept on the park bench. Now they are shadows of Bonnie, Sarah, Kaylob and myself.

PART 3

THE ANTIQUE CLOCK

— 1 —

The Beginning

The year is 1975 in a small suburb called Plainsville, New Jersey, and it is nearing Christmas Day.

My name is Scott Anderson, I was born and raised in a city called Syracuse, New York. After high school, I stuck around there for a few years, watching and waiting for more job opportunities to become available. I worked for a small factory that I knew wasn't going to give me much hope financially for a better future.

One day, as I was waiting in line at a small coffee shop, I overheard a man talking about the huge factory in Plainsville that supplied and made many different parts for all the airline companies in America. He said that the company needed more machinists and this was what I was good at doing.

I got my coffee and went to the table where the man sat, to talk to him. He told me to contact the company as they might be willing to hire me. I did, and within a couple of hours I heard back from them, telling me to come there for an interview.

My wife and I hadn't been married very long, and so this was going to be a big change for both of us if we did move. Cheyenne, my wife, told me to do what I thought was best, and she would agree to whatever the decision was. She had worked in the secretarial field and knew that she could get a job anywhere.

That day, after kissing Cheyenne goodbye as she left for work, I was on my way here to Plainsville, to talk to the boss and CEO of the company. Within an hour I had been hired on at this company, with not just the title of being their machinist, but also one of their supervisors as well.

I called Cheyenne and told her to give notice as we were moving to New Jersey.

That was thirty years ago.

It wasn't long after that when my best friend, Bob Carpenter, was also hired. He and his wife Marie bought a nice home like we did, in a quiet neighborhood west of town. They live two doors down from us. With his wife and mine, we continued to see each other at work and whenever we could outside of work.

Cheyenne had planned a Christmas party for tonight that not only included the neighbors, but also people that we both worked with and for. She was very good at entertaining, and this was something that we did every year just before Christmas.

As I was upstairs dressing for the occasion, Cheyenne came to let me know that most of our guests had arrived, and to adjust my tie. You would think that a man who could build big expensive parts for many airlines could arrange a simple tie, but this was not the case, and something that Cheyenne was good about doing for me.

"Scott, most of our guests have arrived," she announced.

"Okay, good. Did Mr. Thompson and his wife arrive yet?" I asked.

"Not yet, Scott, but you know how he and his wife like to make a grand entrance. I can't wait to see what she wears this year. Last year her dress was so short that I thought every man at the party would go blind from staring at her with disturbing thoughts whenever she bent over.

I still can't believe how Mr. Thompson would allow her to show up here dressed like that," Cheyenne said, laughing.

"Now, Cheyenne, remember that she is our guest, and I doubt that she will hit the sauce as hard this year as she did last year. As for her attire, it is anyone's guess what she will be wearing. She is younger than Mr. Thompson and he probably likes the way she dresses. I know that a lot of men I work with do," I said with a slight chuckle.

"That is funny, Scott. I better get back downstairs where our guests are."

"I will be down shortly," I replied.

"Okay," Cheyenne said as she closed the bedroom door.

I had returned to the bathroom to straighten my hair and then I, too, was walking out of the bedroom and down the stairs to greet our guests.

Cheyenne had gone to the kitchen to inform the caterers to make sure they kept the food and drink coming as I made my way to the punch bowl.

Clark Todd and his wife Charlotte approached me. "I love the way you decorated your home for the holidays, Scott," Clark said as he dunked his cup into the punch bowl.

"Thank you, Clark. Cheyenne and I worked for hours on it. Christmas is our favorite holiday of the year."

"Ours too. This year, Charlotte and I will be all alone as our son and daughter-in-law are going to Hawaii."

"That's nice, Clark. If you want, you are welcome to come here for Christmas dinner. Cheyenne always cooks a bunch of food and loves having company," I replied.

"Thank you, Scott. We will give it some thought."

The doorbell sounded and I went to answer it. Mr. Thompson and his wife, Carey, had arrived. He had made his grand appearance and Carey had outdone herself this year. She had bleached her hair and was now a blonde, wearing an even shorter dress than she had worn last year, with a dark mink coat over it. She was also wearing so much diamond jewelry that her wrists and neck twinkled brighter than the Christmas tree.

She took off her coat and shoved it at Mr. Thompson, who hung onto it, but looked around the room to find a place to put it. Then she went straight to the punch bowl, where she started talking to Clark and Charlotte. I took the coat from Mr. Thompson, to hang it up, as he was still looking around the room, wondering where he could stash it until he had to take Carey home from all the drinking she would be doing that night. He thanked me and started walking in the direction of his wife.

I shut the front door and continued to mingle with the other guests. I could see that everyone there was having a good time. Cheyenne had soft Christmas music playing, and had put a lot of preparation into the menu of food that was being served to our guests.

Cheyenne had them serve finger sandwiches, shrimp and mango skewers, won ton crisps, pineapple-manchego, and spinach and artichoke dip with tiny crackers.

As the night progressed, Mr. Thompson's wife, Carey, became louder and more friendly with the men who worked for her husband, so it was time for Mr. Thompson to take her home and put her to bed. She had been hitting the sauce worse than she had last year.

By midnight, everyone had either left or was leaving. When the last guest had gone, I shut and locked the door.

"Wow, what a party!" Cheyenne said.

"It turned out great as usual, Cheyenne. Again, you outdid yourself."

"Thank you, Scott. I had to turn my head and laugh silently to myself when Mr. Brown's toupee fell in the punch bowl. I know he was embarrassed and I tried not to let him see that I had noticed it happening."

"I heard some of the women giggling and wondered what they thought was so funny, and now I know," Scott said with a slight chuckle.

"This party was the best one that we have had, Scott. I can't wait to see what next year's is like," Cheyenne said.

"Me too. I will let the caterers out, and then join you upstairs," I replied to Cheyenne as I unplugged the Christmas tree. I had to work the next day and needed some rest.

After locking the door behind the caterers, I heard a knock on the front door. My first guess was that someone had forgotten something and had returned to get it.

When I opened the door, Bob was standing there. "Scott, I am sorry to interrupt, but I am worried about Sharon. She went to the movies with a girlfriend tonight and was supposed to be home by now. When Marie and I got home, she wasn't there," Bob said frantically.

"Did you call her friend's house to see if they were there?"

"Yes, and I was told that Sharon and her friend hadn't been there either. Should I call the police, Scott?" Bob asked.

"Not yet, Bob. I will tell Cheyenne what is going on, and we can go look for her ourselves first."

"I am afraid for her safety, Scott," Bob replied.

"I know you are, Bob, and we will find her," I said in what I hoped was a comforting tone.

At that moment, a car pulled up into Bob's drive. Sharon got out and I could see the blood drain back into Bob's face. "She is safe, Scott."

"I know," I said as I put my hand on his shoulder to show him that I really did care.

Bob walked away and I shut and locked the front door. The party was great, but the night could have turned into a disaster if something had happened to Sharon as she was their only child and was their joy and happiness in life.

I started turning off the lights as I made my way up the stairs to sleep. When I got to the bedroom, I saw that Cheyenne was already asleep. It was time for me to get ready for bed and to allow my mind to drift off to dream land.

Our alarm sounded at 7:00 a.m. and it was going to be another long day at work, so it was "up and at it" for me. Cheyenne, who liked to leave early for her job, was putting on her coat to go out the door when she saw me come down the stairs. She hurried into the kitchen, then came out and handed me a cup of coffee, then gave me a kiss goodbye.

After showering and dressing, it was my turn to leave for work. As I was backing out of my drive, I heard the next door neighbors arguing on the opposite side of my house. They were discussing our party last night and the way that George had behaved.

As Mary yelled at him, she told George that she didn't like the way he had looked at Carey. George was trying to defend himself, and it didn't sound like it was doing him any good. I had to laugh as I knew that he would have a lot of apologizing and explaining to do. This might be the last year that they attended our Christmas party.

I drove two doors down, and Bob was already waiting for me on the curb. "Good morning, Bob," I said as he climbed into my car.

"Good morning, Scott. Thank you for taking me to work today, so Marie could use my car. I am sorry that I was so wound up last night. Sharon and her friend got detained for a while by the State Patrol. There was an accident on Route 5. There are many days when I want her to be little again. Back then I knew where she was at."

I smiled at Bob and said, "It's okay. I am glad that you came over. You were worried with every good right to be. Any time you need me, I am always available for you. I understand about how a teenager can cause parents to worry. Cheyenne's daughter did the same thing to us when she was growing up."

"Kids don't think about what they do to their parents. I remember back in high school how you and I were. We, too, were rascals, Scott," said Bob.

"Yes, we were. I remember all of it. I will never forget the time that we loaded Mr. Seivers' mailbox with rocks, and when he went out to check his mail, they all fell out onto his feet. He was so mad. To this day, I don't know if he knew who did this to him," I said as Bob and I laughed about what we called the "good old days."

We continued to talk about all the things we had done together, whether they were good or bad, until we reached the factory. We had also had a good laugh when I told him that George was in trouble with Mary for spending too much time watching Mr. Thompson's wife at the Christmas party. We both agreed that George would pay for that for a long time to come.

When we entered the building, we saw the men that the main factory had sent there to talk to Mr. Thompson. All of us who were supervisors were included in the meeting.

There were six men there, standing around, ready to start the conversation. The main office wanted certain changes done to raise production, and to make more jobs available within the companies. They wanted us to start making parts for NASA as well.

Bob and I looked at each other, staying quiet and listening to every word spoken.

The man who was talking first was well dressed and was very informative. It was as if he was reaching for the stars and the moon, and wasn't going to stop talking until he had made his suggestions clear to Mr. Thompson. When I looked at Bob, I could see that he also agreed with what the man was talking about.

A Native American man stepped forward. He was of medium build with what appeared to me as having a soft-spoken demeanor about him. He, too, was dressed nicely like the other five men standing there. His words were, "The reason why the main company had us come here was not just to tell you that they wanted to increase productivity and growth in this facility, but also to remind you that going forward there will be changes in not just our country, but others all over the world. In other words, we can sit on our hands and do nothing to add to our companies, or we can accept the fact that times are changing and moving forward at a fast pace. This we have no control over."

Mr. Thompson, who was a smart man, stood there looking at all six of the men. He didn't like change, but in this situation he knew that he wasn't the deciding vote. Yes, he could have argued, but he knew how much his wife, Carey, loved money and nice things that twinkle and shine. He also knew that he was replaceable, just like all of us were. So, with him looking at each of the men who stood before him, he told them that he would get his men to prepare the factory for more equipment for the change that was going to take place. The future of our country was going to take everyone in a new direction.

It was a long day, and Bob and I had spent hours helping the other workers start the process of moving and making room for all the new equipment that was about to come there.

The drive home was spent talking to Bob about everything that had taken place that day. We both agreed that the main office was doing the right thing. Advancements were being made, and if they didn't jump on the bandwagon, they would be left behind.

After dropping Bob off, I drove to the house to rest for the remainder of the day. Cheyenne had supper ready, and we sat and talked about what all had happened during the day.

"Scott, I have errands to run tomorrow afternoon when I get off work," she said. "I may not be here when you get home. Is there anything that you need me to do before I return?"

"No, Cheyenne. It is going to be a long day again for me at work. Do what you need to do, and I will meet you back here. Don't worry about fixing supper as I will pick something up for us on my way home. It's late and we both have a huge day waiting for us in the morning, so let's just go to bed and get a good night of sleep."

— 2 —

Questions and No Answers

Morning came fast and it wasn't long after Cheyenne and I went downstairs that we were out the door and on our way to work.

It was almost Christmas, and in a few days we both would be enjoying time off. Tomorrow night was the company Christmas party. Even though Bob and I had agreed to the change at the factory, there were many men working there that hadn't. It would be interesting to see how many of the workers and supervisors showed up for the party with their families. There was no doubt that there would be an extra work load for all of us, but with this would come a raise in our pay.

As I drove to work, the snow really started coming down. I saw people who had slid off the road from the ice that had formed on the highway. The winter months in Plainsville were brutal, and cold. I was worried for Cheyenne's safety, even though I knew that in thirty years of living in New Jersey, she had learned and mastered the safest routes to and from her job. As for me, it was a piece of cake.

Another day at work to watch and listen to all the complaints of many workers. I was sure that the new year would bring a bunch of changes to not only the productivity, but also who still had a job there.

After many hours, I pulled into my driveway. Cheyenne's car was there and I could smell supper from the garage. She forgot I was picking up takeout. When I entered the back door, I saw her putting a clock on the wall. I could see that it was an antique and was curious about it.

"I'm glad you made it home safely," I said.

"The highway was really bad, Scott. I thought about turning around a few times and coming home, but just kept going instead," Cheyenne replied.

"Where did you buy the clock?" I asked.

"I found it at an antique shop close to the same restaurant that we used to eat out at regularly, across town. I had to take care of some business around the area and when I saw the shop, I went in to see what they had.

"It's funny how a person can drive past a building many times and not notice it until today," she continued. "It was old and run down, but my curiosity got the best of me, so I pulled my car over to the curb in front of the store and walked inside. The store was packed with many items. As I was looking around, I noticed this clock sitting in a corner of the room.

"After I walked over to it, to take a better look, I felt a slight tap on my shoulder. When I turned around, I saw an old bearded man. I was startled as I didn't see anyone in there when I entered, and hadn't heard him walk up to me.

"When I did see him, I asked him if he was the owner of the shop. He told me he was, and I told him that I was interested in the clock that he had set in the corner of the room. He told me that it was very old, that he had used it for years, but that he didn't need it any longer. So I bought it. He told me that he had the dial set to where it needed to be, and not to touch or move it. I assured him that I wouldn't, and that it would just be a showpiece in my house on the wall.

"The old man said to be careful with it. To be honest, Scott, he kind of gave me the creeps. I know that this clock is a showpiece, just mainly to look at, but I wondered why he had gone into so much detail about everything. I picked it up and started walking toward the front door to leave the building, and turned around to thank him. Once again, this man no longer was there.

"At that moment, I assumed he may have had a connecting room that I wasn't aware of, so I turned around and walked out of the shop and to my car, and carefully set it on the seat."

"I can see how old it is, Cheyenne. They don't even make clocks like this any longer. If this would have happened to me, I too would have felt strange and creepy," I replied.

"Another thing that amazed me about the shop was that a couple of weeks ago, I took your shirts to the dry cleaners, and had walked right past it, not seeing it. I guess it's strange how sometimes we don't see things that we want or need in our life," Cheyenne said as she dusted off the clock.

When I walked to the kitchen to get a cup of coffee, I reminded Cheyenne about the company Christmas party that Mr. Thompson has every year for the workers and their families.

"Remember that tomorrow night, after I get home, we need to start getting ready for the party. I don't want us to be the first ones arriving, but not the last ones either."

"All right, Scott. Once again, it is going to be interesting to see what Carey wears to her own party," Cheyenne said with a slight snicker.

"This is true, Cheyenne," I replied.

Cheyenne told me about her day at work and I told her about mine as we sat down to eat. Soon after we had cleared the table and put the remaining food away, we were again headed upstairs to sleep.

As I lay in bed, waiting to fall asleep, I kept hearing a strange noise coming from downstairs. I knew that the doors were locked and that no one could walk into our home, but at one instance I heard footsteps coming from the living room.

Quietly, I walked down the stairs, to see what it was I was hearing. Checking every room, including the room downstairs that I used for projects that I worked on, I could see no one in the house. As I came up from the basement, I heard a sound again, and this time it was coming from outside. A branch had fallen from the storm and was hanging against the house. This had to be what had frightened me.

Wanting to laugh and feeling rather stupid at the same time, I made my way through the living room to go back up the stairs to the bedroom. As I passed the old clock, I saw a little light come on at times that seemed to flash. This was something that I had never seen with a clock before. What kind of a clock was this, and what did Cheyenne get herself into by bringing it home?

Because I knew what I thought caused the noise downstairs, I walked back up toward the bedroom, thinking that this was very unusual and I wanted to know more about this clock.

Tomorrow was the Christmas party, but the day after, when I got off of work, I was going to find the shop and ask questions of my own. Was there something more to this antique that we should be aware of, and had Cheyenne accidentally touched the dial when she was dusting it off? All of this would need to wait for a couple of days.

With all of the instructions given by that old man, there was no way either Cheyenne nor myself was going to touch anything on it until I had spoken with the guy.

The next morning, I was up before Cheyenne. As I sat at the living room table, drinking coffee, she made her way down the stairs.

"I am surprised that you are up before me, Scott. Did you sleep last night?" she asked.

"Yes, I did, but it took awhile. You passed out right away, but before I went to sleep, I heard a noise down here and came down to check on it. The noise turned out to be a tree branch that had broken from the storm that we got, and it was hitting against the house. I will take care of it before I leave for work today."

Then I told her, "When I was walking through the living room to return to bed, I noticed that the clock was flickering or flashing. This seemed really strange to me. Did the man that sold this to you mention anything about that?"

"No, Scott. He just said that he had everything set to where it was supposed to be, and not to touch the dial. I might have accidentally bumped it yesterday when I was dusting it off."

"Well, this is the way it has to be until we know for sure what caused it. Neither one of us is going to go near it or touch it. I have some questions and concerns about it, and until I go back to the shop where you got it, and talk to that guy, we are both going to leave it alone," I replied with a somewhat firm tone.

"Okay. I will leave it alone, and also stay away from it," Cheyenne replied.

"This is for the best, as there has to be a reason why it flickered or flashed. Maybe one that neither one of us wants to know about, but I am set on finding out about it," I commented.

This was the end of that conversation as it had turned to the plans for the evening at the party. When Cheyenne left for work, I took my saw and cut the branch down before I left.

It seemed like there were many surprises happening, and some of them were very unexplainable. At the plant we all continued to work to get ready for the new equipment that was scheduled to arrive a few days after Christmas. Some of the workers were still complaining and saying that the main office should have gotten other workers in there to move everything around to their specifications.

Mr. Thompson was handing out Christmas bonuses

to all of us, and these men *still* were complaining. With this happening, I had to remind the men under me that they were replaceable, and that I was capable of doing just that, if need be. Hopefully, this would shut them up.

When the whistle blew, it was time to leave and return home to get ready for the party. I still had the Christmas spirit, but this year felt different than past years.

Before Cheyenne and I left the house, I broke my own rule. I had told Cheyenne that neither one of us were going near the clock until after I had a chance to talk to the old man, but I found myself drawn to it. As I looked at it better, I saw not just the time, but also the year and date on the dial outside of it. Yes, this was unique, but something wasn't right with it.

Cheyenne came down the stairs, ready to leave, so we walked out the door to make our way to Mr. and Mrs. Thompson's house.

When we arrived at the party, many people were already there. When Mr. Thompson answered the door, he said, "Scott, we didn't think you and Cheyenne were coming."

"Why is that? We should be about on time," I replied.

"Do you know what time it is?" Mr. Thompson asked.

"Yes, it should be around 7:30," I said.

"Scott, it is after 10:00."

Surprised, I said, "We looked at our clock before we left, and it said 7:00."

"Scott, I think you need to get a new clock."

I looked at Cheyenne and she looked at me. Something again was very strange about that old clock. Neither one of us had touched it since she placed it on the wall and dusted it. It was like the clock had a mind of its own and changed times whenever it wanted to. This was even more reason for me to talk to the man at the shop.

So I apologized to Mr. Thompson for being so late, and we went inside to make our appearance.

This party was no different than ours, as his wife was still hitting the sauce and laughing way too loud. Bob noticed that I had something on my mind. He came over to me and asked if things were all right.

"Are you and Cheyenne all right?"

"Yes, Bob. Cheyenne bought a new antique clock from a shop a couple of days ago, and we made a mistake trusting it for the correct time," I responded. "That is why we were late getting here. I am either taking it back or going to the shop to talk to the man who sold it to her, to ask questions."

"Well, Scott, you really didn't miss much. It is a nice party and all, but Mr. Thompson and his wife have been bickering off and on all evening. This year's party here isn't near as good as last year's. I think Carey is wondering if her husband will still have a job this time next year, and with this is coming some friction between them. This is a big step for the main office to take, and all of us here know that she likes trinkets and nice clothes. Maybe your clock did you a favor by making you late, so you didn't have to listen to them," Bob said quietly, chuckling.

"Maybe, Bob. Tomorrow night, after I get off work, I am going to the antique shop. Last night when I returned home and saw Cheyenne putting it on the wall, I had an eerie feeling about it. It is very old. I don't know what kind of history it has to it, but there were a lot of stipulations that the old man gave Cheyenne before she bought it. There is a dial at the bottom of it that tells the year. Apparently, the time is not reliable, as we were late getting here. He told her to be careful with it, as he had it adjusted to where it needed to be at now. Also, he said to not bump it, and that he didn't need it any longer. With all of this being said, it makes me wonder exactly what this clock was used for, or where it has been.

"Last night when I went to bed, I heard a strange noise coming from downstairs. I went to check it out and it was a tree branch that was knocking against the house.

It had broken off because of the bad storm outside. That relieved my mind, but when I walked back past the clock, I noticed it flickering or flashing, and I felt very uncomfortable. I have never seen a clock do this before. I have many questions in my mind right now to ask the guy. Hopefully, he will still be open when I get there tomorrow after work."

"That is strange, Scott. Are you sure that the flickering, or flashing, didn't come from the tree decorations, a car that was passing, or a street light outside by the road?"

"I thought of that, Bob, but with the tree being unplugged and across the room from the clock, it couldn't be that. I didn't hear any car passing the house, and the decorations on the pole outside are always away from the front window. So, no, it couldn't have been any of this."

"I think you are right then by going to the guy to see if he knows what caused all of this, " Bob replied. "There has to be a logical answer for it, or should I say, hopefully there is one."

"We will see," I said as Bob and I walked away to join Cheyenne and Marie.

Fortunately for Cheyenne and me, the caterers were still serving food. We had missed the dinner. It appeared that Mr. Thompson was acting jittery as he was probably wondering what Carey was going to do next. They had stopped arguing, but he was following her around and trying to get her to behave with not only her drinking, but also with the flirting that she liked to do.

At 11:30 many of the workers and their wives had already started saying their good-nights and were filing out the door. I guess they had had enough fun for the evening. It was getting late for Cheyenne and myself, as well as the fact that there was work again in the morning. So we, too, were ready to leave. Bob and Marie had already left.

"I apologize again for us being late tonight," I said to Mr. Thompson. "It was caused from a clock that was purchased that gave us the wrong time."

"I understand, Scott. Sometimes things are unavoidable. We are just happy that you and Cheyenne did come for the length of time that you did."

"It was a great party, and we can't wait until next year as we will be on time," I said and laughed.

"Okay, Scott. Thanks again," Mr. Thompson said as he walked us to the door.

I wasn't sure if he believed me, but at that time I didn't care. My mind was set on what all I was going to find out about the old clock that seemed to have a mind of its own.

When we returned home, neither Cheyenne nor myself went anywhere near it. At the moment, it wasn't flickering or flashing. Our inner time clock told us that we needed to go to bed.

— 3 —

Unknown Mystery

After saying goodbye to each other the next morning, it was time for us to make our way through morning traffic to work. This was going to be another hectic day with, at the moment, too much on my mind.

As I drove to work, I wondered if maybe the man that said what he did to Cheyenne and sold her the clock was in some mysterious way warning her, and letting her know what the clock was capable of doing ... or was all of this just a figment of my imagination? Maybe the clock was just broken. This day was going to be one that, later, would give me a lot of answers I really needed.

With the big trucks coming in to deliver all the different equipment that we needed, to not only make airplane parts, but also parts for NASA, the day went fairly fast. The workers had finally calmed down and quit complaining. For once during the entire process of change within the company, they actually pitched in and really wanted to work.

After I left the factory, I was on my way to the west side of town to discuss the clock with the old man. Cheyenne had said that the store was close to the restaurant, so I was driving slowly to find it. I saw an old building that didn't have a sign on it, and stopped to see if this was the right place.

When I walked to the door to open it, the entrance was locked. I looked through the windows to see if maybe the man might be in there. All I saw were cobwebs and no items sitting or laying around inside. I walked to the back of the building, where I proceeded to look around, and all I saw was rubble lying on the ground. Amongst the rubble was a big rusted sign that said, "Westside Antiques."

Since no one was there and the building itself looked like it had been abandoned for years, I drove back to the restaurant, to see if anyone in there could tell me anything about it.

When I entered the restaurant, the girl behind the counter set her cleaning rag down and came over to help me. "I will show you to a table," she said.

"I am not here to eat. I just have a question to ask you."

"Oh, okay."

"Can you tell me anything about the antique shop across the street?"

"Not really, as I am new here, but I will find someone that can," she replied.

The lady walked away, and soon after, a short, older man wearing an apron came out to talk to me.

"Hello, my name is Tim. Can I help you with something?"

"Yes, my wife bought a clock in the antique shop a few days ago from an old man that owned it." I replied. "I went there to ask some questions, and the building appears to be vacant now. Can you tell me if there is another antique shop close by here, or if they moved into another building?"

"No, there isn't another one on this street, and as far as I know, there isn't one anywhere around town."

"This is strange, as she just bought the clock from there."

"Maybe she bought it at a different store other than there, as I have lived and worked around here for thirty-five years, and that building has been shut down for several years. The man who owned it left town years ago. His wife and him got a divorce and he closed it down. I am not sure, but think that she is still somewhere around here. I don't know her name, but she would be the one to contact about it," the man commented.

"Okay, I will try to find her. Thank you for your time," I said as the man started walking back to the kitchen.

This was really weird now as Cheyenne knew where she had gotten the clock. The only thing left to do was get into my car and go home.

Cheyenne was waiting for me when I walked through the door. "Did you find the shop okay, Scott?"

"I think I did, but the one I went to looked like it had been closed for some time. I looked through the windows and all I saw were cobwebs. The door was locked and there was a huge rubble pile in the back. A sign saying Westside Antiques was the only thing I saw that was worth anything there, and then it was rusted. Is this the place where you went?"

"Yes, that was the name of the store. Did you ask anyone about the store, Scott?" Cheyenne had a confused look on her face.

"After I left there, I went to the restaurant and talked to a man from their kitchen. He told me that the place had been out of business for many years, and that as far as he knew, there wasn't another antique shop anywhere in town. Many years ago, the man that owned it closed the store after he and his wife divorced. He suggested that I contact her about it. This is way too spooky for me."

"Scott, I know where I was at, and this whole thing doesn't make sense to me either. What do we do now?"

"I believe you, Cheyenne. I agree that this is very unusual and weird. I know there has to be an explanation for it, and tomorrow, since I don't work, I am going to go to the library to look up some information on the old shop and the man that owned it. Maybe I can find out his wife's name and then talk to her about it. Let's try hard not to let our minds get too much out of control for now. Just don't touch the clock," I reminded her in a firm tone.

That night was interesting as Cheyenne kept looking at the clock from across the room. For me, I was waiting for the clock to flash, and for her it was out of wonderment and thinking that for some odd reason she was in the twilight zone, or that this all was just a dream.

When Cheyenne went to bed, I continued to sit in the dark, watching the clock to see what it did next. About midnight, I once again saw it flash. There were no cars on our street, and no Christmas tree lights on. *How strange is this?* I thought. I got up from my chair and walked over to it. I thought about taking it off the wall and hauling it outside to the trash dumpster, and then I changed my mind. This clock was important to Cheyenne or she wouldn't have bought it, so I left it on the wall and went upstairs to bed. Tomorrow would tell the story when I went to the library. If not, then I would make a decision on what to do with it.

As I lay in bed, once again I heard noises coming from downstairs. Instead of getting up and going to check it out, I attributed it to being another branch hitting the house. I knew our home wasn't haunted, and that this had to be an easy fix with the clock.

Maybe the man I talked to at the restaurant didn't know what he was talking about. Maybe the cobwebs were already there and Cheyenne hadn't noticed them when she went into the store. Another man, other than the original owner, could have bought the store and then, after Cheyenne left, decided that he should close it as nothing else was good enough to sell. Maybe the clock was just broken. All of this could happen, and I refused to believe otherwise, at least for now.

Convincing myself that everything was just fine, I was finally able to go to sleep. When I opened my eyes in the morning, Cheyenne was already downstairs making sausage and eggs for breakfast. Bob had come over and was sitting at the table. Cheyenne had asked him to stay and eat with us, and he said yes. Marie had gone shopping and he wanted to know how things had gone at the antique store last night.

"There he is," Bob said as I walked down the stairs in my pajamas and bathrobe.

"Good morning, Bob. What brings you here so early?" I asked.

"Scott, it is 10:00, and to me that isn't early," Bob replied with a chuckle.

"Wow, I must have really been tired to have slept that long," I replied.

"I came over to see what that guy had to say."

"Well, Bob, the weirdest thing that I ever had happen to me so far occurred yesterday."

"Tell me more, Scott," said Bob.

"I went to the west side of town, looking for this place, and found the building across the street down some from the restaurant that Cheyenne and I liked to go to when we first moved here. The building was very old and looked run down with some boards hanging off of it. I tried to go inside, but the door was locked. I stepped to the side and looked through windows to see if anyone was in there. The place was empty. The only thing I saw was a bunch of cobwebs. I then went around back to see if maybe there was an unlocked back door. Instead, I found rubble with a fairly big sign that said Westside Antiques. The rubble was nothing but junk, and the sign was rusted as if it had been sitting out in the weather for quite a while.

"Then I decided to go to the restaurant and ask about the place, to see if maybe there was an antique shop close by and I was at the wrong one, or if maybe the man that owned the place had taken the good stuff out of there and moved to a different building.

"The man in the restaurant told me that the place had been closed down for many years and that he didn't know where the owner was, but he suggested that I contact the man's ex-wife, to see if she could tell me anything about it.

"I thanked him for his time and left. Cheyenne told me that I had gone to the right place, and so my next move is to go to the library today and look up some information about it from years ago, when the man I talked to said that it was in business. Maybe I can find out the name of the guy's wife at the time and find her. This clock has turned into a real mystery as it seems to have a mind of its own.

"Last night, after Cheyenne went to bed, I stayed down here for a while, and again the clock flashed or flickered. Now, I am not sure if I am making more out of this than needs to be, or if it is just broken. Also, the worst thing bothering me is that Cheyenne walked into this store, talked to the owner, who took her money, and walked out of there and nothing was strange to her about the building, except for the creepy old man that tapped her shoulder and said he was the owner.

"I keep repeating over and over again in my head what he told her about the clock. None of this, Bob, is making any sense to me," I said with a confused look.

"I don't blame you for being confused, Scott. There has to be a mistake. A building doesn't look like that in a few days' time, and the sign doesn't rust that quickly. Also, Cheyenne wouldn't make up a story about where she bought the clock. I know that I, too, haven't ever heard a story like this one before. As for the clock itself, I suppose it might be broken. If you can't find out anything at the library, Scott, it might be worth it to take it apart and check it out, to see if there is something loose which could be where the flickering is coming from," said Bob.

"That's true. I hadn't thought about that. If it is, then that would explain the misreading of it the night of the company party. Thanks, Bob. That gives me some hope and encouragement."

Cheyenne walked back into the living room from the kitchen and I didn't want to spook her. She was a little skittish about what the clock had been doing anyway, and I was sure she had questions of her own that she would like to have answered.

She had not only brought scrambled eggs, sausage and hash browns, but toast and a big pot of coffee. We all sat there and ate, and then Bob announced that he had to go home to repair the boards that had come off from the horrible wind storm on his fence.

Cheyenne and I continued to sit at the table, drinking more coffee.

"I hope you can find out something at the library today, so we know about the clock and also what to do with it," Cheyenne commented.

"Me too. They always have large books in there that have every business listed and usually they give a reason why the store shut down, or if it is still in business elsewhere. By the time I get back, I will know something, I am sure."

Cheyenne cleared the dishes and told me that she had to go shopping just like Marie, and that she would see me later. Again, a small kiss goodbye and she was on her way out the front door to leave for a while. I would see her later.

It was my turn to get ready for my day and a trip into town. Being that New Jersey weather was blowing, snowing and very cold, the traffic was light, so it was easier to drive without so many traffic jams or cars slowing down because of the bad roads.

After I parked my car, I walked up the steps to the library and opened the door. There was an elderly woman wearing glasses that had slid down some on her nose. I asked her where I could find the book that would tell about antique buildings in or close to the area.

She instructed me where to go, and so I walked to the back, where I found a long table and a huge book with all the names of businesses that had been, and still existed, in the town. It also showed pictures of them and a story that went with each one. As I paged through it, I came across "Westside Antiques."

The information that it gave was dated back 80 years ago. At that time, the building was new and the sign was placed on top of the shop. The article said that the building belonged to Mr. and Mrs. Ryan Lockhart. It also told that because of unexplainable acts that had happened in the store, the shop was closed forty years ago.

I kept reading. The article said that Mr. Lockhart appeared to be missing shortly after the shop closed, and his wife refused to give the town permission to tear down the building.

There was no explanation on what the unexplainable acts were, and it didn't tell the first name of Mrs. Lockhart. If she was still alive, she would be very old by now, and depending on her health situation, she may not even remember the old shop.

I closed the book and walked to the front desk, where I asked the woman sitting behind the desk if I could borrow their phone directory. Of course, she told me that I could, and I opened it to look for any last name of Lockhart that was listed. I found one and wrote down the address and phone number. When I returned home, I would try to call the number and see if I could go there to talk to the person listed.

Before I left, I made a copy of the picture that it showed of the building and the article that was below it. I needed verification from Cheyenne once again that this was the same building that she had been in when she bought the clock.

When I was finished, I thanked the librarian for the use of the phone directory, and walked back to my car.

It was Christmas Eve, and I had become obsessed with wanting to find answers, but was willing to wait a couple of days in order to enjoy Christmas with Cheyenne before resuming my venture of the unknown behavior of the clock.

— 4 —

More Questions

A s I was driving down our street to go home, I saw Bob
unloading a Christmas tree off the top of his car. I
pulled over to the curb. He saw me stopping and came to
the window to talk to me.

"How did it go at the library, Scott?" he asked.

I grabbed the printouts of the building with the information on them and showed him what I had found out.

"This is what the building used to look like many
years ago, Bob. It is a wreck now."

Bob read the paper and then replied, "Now you have
the name of the owners, and maybe with that, you can get
the information you need about the clock."

"Mr. and Mrs. Lockhart would be extremely old, if
they are still alive. I am hoping that the name listed in the
phone directory is a relative of theirs and can help. I am
really curious as to how this mystery is going to play out,
Bob."

"Me too, Scott. I am wondering what the unexplainable things that took place are," said Bob, laughing.

"Merry Christmas, my friend. It is time for me to go
home and fill Cheyenne in on everything that I want to do.
Then I need to put it all out of my mind for a couple of
days. I don't want to consume Cheyenne with this as it is
Christmas."

"Merry Christmas, Scott. Eventually the truth will
be known about the clock. Please tell Cheyenne that both
Marie and myself wish her a merry Christmas as well,"
Bob replied.

"I will, and the same for Marie as well."

I drove two doors down and into my drive. When I entered the house, Cheyenne was there, but dressed in something that looked like it was dated back years before either she or I were born.

"Nice dress, Cheyenne. Where did you get that?" I asked.

"I found it in my closet, Scott. It fits perfectly and tonight I thought I would wear it. I haven't seen it before and, to be honest, I don't remember buying it."

"It looks nice on you, but I have never seen you wear your hair up the way it is fixed," I replied.

"For some reason, I feel like I have worn it this way before. Even the shoes I am wearing are something that I can't remember buying." Then she asked, "Did you go to the library?"

"Yes, and these are the papers I printed out on the building. I want you to look at the picture and verify again that this is the same place that you went to the other day," I said as I handed her the pages.

Cheyenne looked at the pages and read what was on them. "Scott, this is the same building I went to."

"I know, and I am not questioning you on anything. After Christmas I will see if the phone number that I have is still working, and also if I can go talk to the person it belongs to. It's Christmas Eve, and so I want to concentrate on Christmas and forget about the clock for now. Whatever this is will more than likely turn out to be something very explainable, and then we will get the clock fixed so that it works again."

"Okay, Scott," Cheyenne agreed.

Our night progressed and I still wondered why Cheyenne had come downstairs wearing a really old dress and shoes with her hair piled on top into a bun. This was not like her at all.

"Scott, I feel pretty with the floral design and lace around my neck and sleeves," Cheyenne said as she twirled around. "It is so long."

"It's a nice dress, but it looks like a dress that I wouldn't think you would wear or like," I responded.

Once again she said, "I don't remember buying it or the shoes. Then again, I feel like I am not remembering many things the last few days. Today I forgot my handbag when I went to town. I came back for it after I got to the store. Yesterday I forgot to grab my house key. When I got home, I had to crawl through a window that I didn't get completely closed to get into the house. There is something wrong with me," Cheyenne replied in a confused voice.

"No, there isn't. It is just the clock. It has had both of our minds consumed for days now, and like I said, for now we are just going to enjoy Christmas and tonight. Yes, you do look pretty in that dress," I said, trying hard to comfort her and also to give her a compliment.

"Thank you, Scott."

After she did her twirls in the living room again, she went to the kitchen to prepare supper for us. Her actions had me concerned as she hadn't ever worn anything like that before, and her forgetting things was not like her at all. She was the one to remind me about things. I would continue to watch her and see if I noticed anything else that was strange about her. As badly as I didn't want to think it or feel it, my mind kept returning to the antique clock that was giving off some kind of a signal that could have changed her, along with her mood swings. Or again, it could all be coincidental.

The rest of the evening we sat around and looked at the lights on our tree and relived many Christmas Eves that we'd had together, plus other memories.

I believed that everything was back to normal, and then when it was time to go to bed, she informed me that she would take off the shoes, but wanted to wear the dress to bed. This was very strange and unusual behavior for her. She left her hair piled on top of her head and laid down on the bed. I told her that I understood, but I wasn't really understanding, and I laid in bed, watching and wondering what would come next.

Around 2 a.m. Cheyenne got up out of bed and started twirling around again, singing some kind of song that I was not familiar with. When she had finished the song, she lay down in bed again and went back to sleep.

I continued to watch her, and finally I was so tired, I went to sleep.

Christmas morning, when I woke up, I didn't see Cheyenne in bed and, being worried about her, I rapidly got out of bed to go looking for her. I practically ran down the stairs to find her sitting at the table, drinking coffee.

"Cheyenne, are you all right?" I asked.

"Yes, Scott, why wouldn't I be?" she asked.

"I just thought I would ask. Good morning and Merry Christmas," I replied.

"Merry Christmas to you too. I woke up this morning wearing something that my grandmother would have worn. I don't know where I got it, or don't even remember putting it on before I went to bed. I am surprised that you let me go to bed in something like that," Cheyenne said.

"It's okay, Cheyenne. You might have been half asleep when you got ready for bed last night." I wanted to tell her about how she had been wearing it when I got home yesterday, about the twirling and saying she was so pretty, and how she loved the dress and the shoes, which I was sure she hadn't discovered yet on the floor, not to mention the hair still piled on top of her head. I didn't tell her that she had also wanted to wear the dress to bed. Instead, I decided that this was a conversation for another day. For now she appeared to be normal, and we both wanted to enjoy Christmas Day.

Cheyenne had already started cooking and our dinner was going to be very good. I hadn't heard anything from Clark and his wife as to whether they were coming over for Christmas dinner, so I assumed that they had different plans.

We went into the living room and unwrapped some presents under the tree, and Cheyenne put on her soft Christmas music. This day was going to be a good one as I was making it that way. No talk about the clock.

About 3:30 in the afternoon, the doorbell sounded. When I opened it, Bob and Marie were standing at our door. They had brought us a homemade fruit cake, unlike the ones in the store. Cheyenne handed them a plate of homemade gingerbread men cookies, and we went to the living room to sit and talk.

When Cheyenne and Marie went to the kitchen to get us all some coffee, it gave me a chance to talk to Bob.

"How are things going in the house with the clock?" Bob asked.

"At the moment, I am more concerned about Cheyenne, Bob. Yesterday, when I came through the door, I saw her dressed in an old dress that her grandmother could have worn, and shoes to match. She had her hair piled up on her head in the shape of a bun. This outfit is something she wouldn't be caught dead at her own funeral wearing. She kept saying how pretty she felt, and was turning around in circles.

"When we went to bed, she wanted to wear the dress. I wasn't about to argue with her, so I acted like I didn't care. I was afraid to sleep as I didn't know what was next. Early in the morning, she got up out of bed and started twirling around again and singing, some kind of old song that I didn't recognize. After a while, she returned to bed. By then I was so tired, I fell asleep.

"Things around here have really been strange, as this morning she commented on how she thought she might be losing her mind as she has been forgetting little things and wondering why she put on an old dress to wear to bed that she didn't even remember buying. I never told her that she wore it before she went to bed, nor what she had done after she went to sleep.

"With everything that is happening around here, the

mystery of the clock is becoming an obsession in not just my mind, but from what I saw, Cheyenne's mind as well."

"Wow, Scott!! I don't know what to say! This is one story I am going to keep to myself. Marie and Cheyenne are very good friends, as you and I are, and I don't want Marie accidentally bringing any of this up, as it would only make Cheyenne wonder more about what she is doing," Bob commented.

"I agree," I replied. "After I have talked to hopefully one of the relatives of the people that owned the store, I will either get answers, or I will try to adjust the clock differently, or I will throw it in the trash. Once again, this may not even be the clock. It just might be circumstantial occurrences that would have happened even if the clock wasn't here."

By then, Cheyenne and Marie had entered the room and all of us sat there and laughed and talked about many other things that we had done together over the many years of being friends.

About 6:00 p.m. Bob and Marie went home. It was going to be another interesting night to see if anything new took place. Cheyenne was acting normal and she had taken the old dress and put it in the garbage while still going on about how she couldn't imagine herself wearing anything like that to bed. I just sat and agreed with her on what she said, and left it at that.

We continued to watch the twinkling lights on the tree and cuddled beside it. The day had gone well, and around midnight we decided that it was time to go to bed. Tomorrow was a day of phone calls, and hopefully answers from anyone that could tell me anything about the clock, the building, and the owners.

— 5 —

Hopefully Answers Given

The next day was Saturday, and no work for us. This would mean a full day of investigation. Cheyenne was doing laundry and planning a trip to town. I went to the laundry room and told her that it was going to be an all-day venture for me. She asked me if I wanted her to come with me, and I told her that it might be best if she didn't. When I returned, I would update her on everything.

I planned on making a call to the number I had gotten at the library. Cheyenne commented that she would keep good thoughts, and hopefully the mystery of the clock and everything weird that had been going on there, would be solved very soon, so that things could get back to normal.

I also told her that I wished for the same thing, and that if I couldn't get the answers I needed, I was going to try to fix the clock myself or take it back to the rubble pile behind the store.

After she agreed with me, I went back into the living room to make the phone call. The phone rang a few times, and then a lady answered. "Hello, Lockharts' residence," she said.

"Hello. My name is Scott Anderson and I would like to talk to someone. Is there a Mr. or Mrs. Lockhart available?" I asked.

"I'm not sure which one you are referring to."

"Is there a Ryan Lockhart there, or his wife?" I clarified.

"No, my mother passed away years ago, and my father, Ryan, turned up missing many years ago. My name is Linda Lockhart. I am their daughter. Can I help you?" she asked.

"What I need to talk to you about will require a visit. Can I come to your home and speak with you?" I asked.

"Sure, that would be fine. I will be home this morning." Linda Lockhart gave me the address.

"Okay. I will see you soon," I said.

After hanging up the phone, I kissed Cheyenne goodbye. Hopefully, this trip wouldn't be a waste of time.

As I drove to the Lockharts' estate, I went over all the questions in my mind so that I would be prepared when I got there. The house was across town in a fancy neighborhood, where only the rich people lived, so I knew exactly where to go.

The traffic again was light and the highway was cleared off, so it wasn't going to take me long to get there.

When I arrived at the huge house on the hill, I walked to her front door and rang the doorbell. A tall man wearing a suit came to the door and opened it. "Can I help you?" the man asked.

"Yes, I am here to speak to Linda Lockhart. She is expecting me," I replied.

"I will see if Madam is available. Come in, please," he said.

I stood there waiting for her to enter the room and looked around at all the fancy things that she had. On the wall was a big portrait of two people. It was one of a man and a woman. I assumed that it was of her mother and father as the portrait was very old and in black and white.

Finally, an older lady came into the room. "Hello. I am Linda Lockhart. Can I be of help to you?" she asked.

"Yes, you can," I said as she escorted me to another room, where she asked me to sit down. In front of us was an antique teapot that appeared very elegant. She poured me a cup of tea, waiting for me to explain to her what the reason for my visit was.

"The story that I am about to tell you might sound

far-fetched, but believe me, it is true," I said. "Days ago, my wife was shopping and she came across your father's antique shop. At the time, she decided to go in and look around, in hopes of buying something.

"While she was in there, an older man came up to her and tapped her on the shoulder. When she turned around, she told him that she was interested in a clock that was sitting in the corner of the room. At that time, he told her that with this clock came instructions. He said that he had the clock set to the right time, and for her not to touch the dial. He said to be careful with it and that he didn't need it any longer.

"Before she walked out of the building, she turned around to thank him and he wasn't there. So she left and took it to our home, to place it on the wall. She dusted it off and since then, I have noticed the clock flickering, or flashing. The clock hasn't kept time as we were late for a party. My wife started forgetting things and the other night, when I came home to her, she was wearing a really old dress that looked like something her grandmother may have worn. She wanted to wear it to bed. Then in the night, she got up and started twirling around, singing an old song.

"In the morning, she didn't remember any of this, and wondered why she had worn something like that old dress to bed, that she didn't remember buying. That day, her hair was piled on top of her head, and she was even wearing old, out-dated shoes. My wife, Cheyenne, is very picky about what she wears and the way her hair looks, and this was not like her at all.

"I have gone downstairs at night after hearing noises, only to find the clock flashing or flickering, and I'm wondering what is causing this. Not knowing if the clock was broken, I went back to the store to talk to your father and ask questions. When I got there, the building was old and run down, with some loose boards hanging from it and cobwebs inside.

"When I looked for a back door to go into, there was none, and instead I found a big rubble of stuff that didn't look like it was worth anything, and the old 'Westside Antiques' sign lying in the rubble. It was rusted and looked like it had been there for quite a while.

"All of this didn't make any sense to me, as my wife had just bought this clock from whom I believe was your father. Still wanting answers, I went to the restaurant across the street, to talk to anyone who might be able to clarify in my mind what had taken place with the building, thinking that maybe Cheyenne had gone to one that had been moved close by and had the same name.

"The man I spoke with told me that the shop had been closed for many years and that there was no other shop in town. By then, my mind was out of control with needing answers, and so I went to the library to look up the store, thinking that maybe the shop wasn't that old, and that the man in the restaurant didn't know what he was talking about.

"This is where I got your phone number from the phone book as the book did tell your dad's name as being the owner. So today I am here, asking you if you can give me the answers that I need," I said as I took a deep breath.

I expected Linda Lockhart to throw me out on my ear, thinking I was crazy, but instead she looked at me calmly and said, "I will tell you what I know, but I have a question for you first. What does the old clock look like?"

"The clock is very old. It appears to have a movement with one winding point located in the center of the dial. To wind the clock with the crank, it would need to be turned to each revolution clockwise. If I know what I am talking about after this is completed, the correct time should be set with the moving of the minute hand, either clockwise or counter clockwise, and if it is running too fast or too slow, it would need to be adjusted by the nut on the bottom of the dial," I told her, hoping that I had given her the information she needed.

"Okay, I am sure now that I know what clock you are referring to. You did a good job explaining this, as when I was very young, I would go to work with my father and at that time he had many different clocks in the store.

"This particular clock came from England many hundreds of years ago. My father bought it from a man who also told him the same thing that the man you said your wife bought it from specified that day. I was very young, but remember that things in the shop started getting weird after my father put the clock in the corner of the store. As you know, the store had just one room and my father said that he liked it that way as it made the store look friendlier and cozy. Many years ago times were different. Most people liked this because everything that my father had to sell was in one room.

"One day when I went to work with my father, he too was cleaning what we had in the store. Father seemed to be infatuated with the clock. He told me that he was connected to it and that it made him feel good about himself, and at times he felt as if it was speaking to him.

"I might have been young, but as I stood next to my father, I couldn't hear anything coming from the clock, but apparently he did. When people came in and wanted to buy it, he would tell them that it wasn't for sale, that it belonged to the store. At that time, Father had placed it on the wall. There would be days that he wouldn't allow me to go to work with him, and when he came home from work, it was like he was a different man. Kind of what you are telling me about your wife.

"My mother and father would argue, and this became more frequent. Mother didn't understand why my father insisted on being at the shop as much as he was. His personality had changed and my brother and myself wondered why, just like our mother did.

"He was obsessed with this old clock. I remember what I, too, believe was a little flicker of some sort once in a while, but being so young, I thought maybe it was just something that the clock did and I never mentioned it to my father.

"One day I noticed my dad adjusting the dial at the bottom of the clock. I assumed that he was maybe cleaning the gears, so that it would be more of a showpiece for the store. So I went outside to play. I had only been gone a few seconds and went back into the store to get my doll that I'd forgotten to grab. When I returned, my father was nowhere in sight. As you know, there isn't a back door and no connecting rooms. There wasn't even a bathroom in the store. I stood there for a minute, wondering where my father had gone as he couldn't have come out the front door as I would have seen him.

"I opened the front door and looked outside, to see if I could see him, even though I was sure that he didn't follow me outside. When I didn't see him, I turned around to wait for him to return, and he was standing in the store. I thought that maybe he might have been on the floor at the time, fixing something, so I once again didn't ask him anything about it.

"That night, my father and my mother got into a huge fight. My father said that if she didn't shut up, he was going to leave her, and there would be no way that she would ever be able to find him. This just didn't upset my mother, it also upset my brother and me. We didn't want our father to leave us.

"Mother, being very mad at him, told him that if he wanted to leave, she didn't care where he went and that she wouldn't try to find him. Things calmed down some, but I could see that Mother and Father were at the breaking point of their marriage.

"Father had changed and the only thing that really mattered to him was the clock. At least this is what my brother and I believed.

"The next day, Father again took both my brother and me to work with him. We stood around in the store, watching people come and go. It was like Father was having a going-out-of-business sale as he lowered the price on everything in there. By the end of the day, the only thing left were items that he really didn't care about. He told us to grab what was left and take it around back and put it in a pile. He went up on top of the store and took down the sign, then put it in the same pile as the other items that had gotten carried there.

"When everything was out of the store, Father told us that he loved us, but that it was time for him to go on a different journey in life, and that he would try hard to come and visit us from time to time. He took us home, but didn't enter the house to tell Mother that he was leaving her for good. He left us standing at the beginning of the drive, crying, and wondering if maybe we were the reason he chose to leave.

"We were way too young to understand any of what had been happening at home or at the store. When Mother heard us crying, she came out to see what was wrong and asked us where Father went. We told her what he had told us, and that we were sorry for making him leave. Mother told us that Father had changed and that we had nothing to do with it, and were not to blame ourselves. She said that she would get in her car and go to the shop and try to talk him into coming home.

"She fired up the old car and drove to the store. When she got there and went inside, the store was completely empty. Even the old clock was gone from the wall and there was no sign of Father. She locked the door and didn't go back.

"The next day, she went to the courthouse and filed for a divorce from my father. At that time, the town was smaller and everyone was looking for him. He was nowhere to be found, and so after a certain length of time, her divorce was over with. If Mother were alive, she could probably tell you more. As for the day that your wife went to the store and bought the clock from that man, I don't know what to say, as he has been gone for many years, and that clock was not in the store. I hope that I have been of help to you, Mr. Anderson."

"You have been, and thank you," I said as I took out the papers that I had printed and showed them to her.

"That is the old store," she said. "The portrait on the wall is that of my mother and father. You are welcome to take it home, to show to your wife, to confirm that the man she spoke to is my father."

"Thank you. I will do that, and then bring it back to you. There has to be an explanation for this. Maybe your father wasn't the one who sold her the clock, and for some reason Cheyenne got confused as to where she was at. She did say that she had been forgetting things," I replied.

"This is true," she said as she walked me to the door after handing me the portrait.

Again I thanked her and went on my way back to the house to talk to Cheyenne about everything that was said.

When I walked through the door, she was waiting for me. I told her the story and watched the color drain from her face. Then I showed her the portrait and asked her if this had been the man who sold her the clock. Again she had a weird look on her face and told me yes, it was.

There was nothing else to do at that moment, but take Cheyenne with me to Linda Lockhart's home and give the portrait back to her.

— 6 —
Answers and Solutions

When we arrived back at the Lockhart estate, Cheyenne went inside with me. She wanted to meet this lady and thank her for all her help that she had given us that day.

"I am sorry to make you relive a time in your life which I know is hard for you to talk about," said Cheyenne. "This whole thing has been a mystery and one that we don't want to live again. I would really like to know what planet I was on that day when I bought the clock, as this is the man in the portrait who sold it to me. If he was still alive, he would have been much older today." Cheyenne felt like biting her tongue for implying that Linda Lockhart's father might be dead.

"It's okay, Cheyenne. This happened so many years ago that by now most of the hurt is gone. When you left, Scott, I went through some old papers that I had forgotten about. These are papers that my mother had left for my brother and me before she passed away, and I found something that could be of interest to you. It might even make you more aware of what you have been experiencing in your home. I am not saying that this paper is true or has the answers that you have been searching for, but I do believe that it will help you."

She went on, "My father was drawn to that clock. As I told you, he bought it from a stranger, just like Cheyenne did. He was not only a business owner, but also a scientist. He believed in many things, and one of the things he believed in was that our world was going to change some-day. He had found something that made him believe this even more so.

"On this paper are drawings, and it also shows a picture of the dial at the bottom—the one that he told Cheyenne not to bump, and to be careful with—as he had it set to where it needed to be. He knew that the clock wouldn't do him any good any longer, and he wanted to sell it to her, in hopes it would bring a better future for her. I believe that when she paid him for it and he walked away, my father went back into time, where he had been all these years. He may have found a way to get there on his own, as he told Cheyenne that he didn't need the clock any longer. So I am going to give you this paper to do with as you choose, and also whatever you do with the clock is your choice as well."

At that moment, she handed me a paper that was yellowed with age, which showed a picture of the clock and the dial. He had made pencil markings on the paper with numbers and other drawings that might have been his graphs. Why he would leave it there for someone to find was a mystery in itself, unless he knew that within time it would be found and figured out. It showed the dial was set at a different year and date than it actually was at that time. This was probably how he could leave the store without Linda—and Cheyenne—seeing him.

I had heard of something called Time Travel, but back then I didn't believe in it, or think it existed. This was far more advanced than the NASA project and parts that we had been working on at the factory. In the future, when our world was safe and more advanced, maybe Time Travel would become familiar to everyone and anyone would be able to experience this without an old antique clock, and somehow Mr. Ryan Lockhart knew this.

At the time, it took him into another period of time where he wanted to be, but for some reason unknown to me, he had returned that day to his old store, to be at when his life was good. Maybe he went to visit Linda and her brother and they didn't even recognize it at the time.

Being convinced that this was what had taken place, and that our future was left up to God, and advancements that our world would eventually discover, I knew exactly what I had to do with the clock. It could be a danger to us, as neither Cheyenne nor myself were qualified to figure it out, and we loved the way our lives had gone so far, and looked forward to a calm, peaceful future of growing old together, without the clock directing our lives through Time Travel.

So I thanked Linda again and told her that I would keep the paper and take the clock to a place where I knew it could be monitored and hopefully understood.

She told me that she was happy to have helped and that this would be for the best, and maybe someday Time Travel could become a reality. She told us that with my coming there that day with the questions and all the answers that we had worked on together to resolve, it had given her the peace she needed to finish out her life on earth.

I told her that I was happy that I had been able to help her as well, and that it looked like the mystery had been solved.

Cheyenne and I left and went home to take the clock down from the wall. We were convinced that it would do nothing but harm us, and we wanted to give it to a place that actually could work with it and figure out what was in it, or about it, that had the power to take someone into a different hemisphere to start a new life, or maybe undo the mess and mistakes that were made in the past one.

We both realized that Mr. Ryan Lockhart was not just a great antique dealer, but also a great scientist who thought at the time that he himself could either control or change the world.

When we walked into the research institute in Marvel, New Jersey, that was filled with many scientists, we handed them the yellowed paper and the clock. Along with this came the stories of our experiences with the clock, and also the ones of Linda Lockhart.

The men who took what we had brought to them, and who had sat down to listen to what we had to say, said that they would all make sure that the clock didn't get into the wrong hands, and that they would experiment with it, but keep everyone safe.

One of the men told me that with the experimentation he would see what made it tick. I knew what he was talking about, but because of his words directed at me, I had to laugh because, of course, a clock *ticks*.

This antique clock had powers that were far more advanced than what a simple supervisor of a factory that made parts for many airlines, or a rocket, would ever be able to figure out.

Finally, Cheyenne and I could breathe again. We left the building and were going home to our dull but wonderful life that we shared and planned to share together for many years to come.

The mystery of the old antique clock had been solved.

PART 4

IS HE OR ISN'T HE?

— 1 —
Is This Guy For Real?

It's mid October and the leaves on the trees are changing to red, orange and lavender. When I came downstairs this morning with my wavy, long brown hair wrapped in a towel, to grab a quick cup of coffee to take upstairs with me as I finished getting ready for work, I happened to look out the kitchen window.

There was a big moving truck that had already arrived at the house across the street, unloading furniture. I watched for a couple of minutes and then returned to the bedroom.

I work at a meat-packing plant in Mission, Utah. I know that my job doesn't have a big fancy title behind it, but what I do there pays the bills and keeps me working.

My name is Karen Albertson. I grew up and went to school in a small town called Mesquite, Nevada. I hung around there for a few years after high school, wondering whether I wanted to spend six or eight more years going to a university, or just get out and find a job that I liked.

After many talks that I had with my parents, I decided that I would try the work force, and work for a while. My parents, of course, were against it. They said that I had artistic talent and they would like to see me further my education. Instead of doing this, I followed my boyfriend at the time to Mission, where I have lived ever since.

It's a small town surrounded by mountains, and this was something that fascinated me from the moment that we arrived here. Within the town are several coal mines, which employ hundreds of men and women. Maybe I might have been able to get a job with one of them, but the thought of going underground with tons of dirt on top of me, not being able to see that well, with maybe a possible cave-in, didn't appeal to me.

When I saw the meat-packing plant outside of town, I decided that for a starter job this would be a good one. I knew that they would pay a decent wage and that the work would be hard, boring, and time-consuming, but at the end of the day I would be going home.

This was five years ago and I am still here. When I started, I didn't have to work with the slaughtering process, and they put me in a large, cold room, packaging meat that was cut. A much cleaner job with more pay than if I had gotten stuck in the other one.

As for my boyfriend that I followed here, that relationship ended. He liked other women way too much, and I wasn't going to deal with that. I moved out of our apartment and into a fairly nice house on Elm Street. It's not in the most expensive part of the town, but it fits into my budget quite well.

That particular day, the plant had put me in charge of training a new man at work. Apparently he had experience, but like with every new job, there are always different rules, and their way of doing things in the work place is always different with many companies. I had trained other people before, so that wouldn't be a problem for me.

When the man came into the break room to apply for a job the other day, I had gone into the office to punch out. The plant assistant was interviewing him at the time. The man was friendly, but there was something about him that made me feel weird. The guy was tall, not bad looking, and when he looked at me, his eyes looked wild. When he spoke to me, he hunched over and wasn't that far away from my face. I guess what it was could have been his demeanor of the way he presented himself.

He kept looking around at everything and acted jittery if someone came through the door. At the time, I threw it off as maybe the fact that he was nervous and curious at what was in the building. Since this is the day that I will be working closely with him, explaining his job, even though I was told that he has done this before, maybe I will have a whole new perspective on how he really is. At least this was what I was hoping for.

My hair turned out great, I was dressed and on my way to work. My house was within minutes of the meat-packing plant, so within fifteen minutes I was driving into the parking lot.

As I entered the building, I saw the man sitting on a chair, waiting for me. With me still watching him and not really liking what I saw, I walked over to him to get him and take him to the office, where he would punch in and out of work on the time clock each day.

From there we went to the room where we sterilized our hands, then got our gowns, hats and long gloves that were needed. Each of us had to wear these before we could even enter the large processing room where we would be working.

"Hello. My name is Karen Albertson. I will be the one training you today," I told him.

"My name is Brian Osborn. I am pleased to meet you," he said as his eyes once again grew large and he leaned over to shake my hand.

"If you want to follow me, I will show you what you do each day before you start packing meat," I said. Again, I had a weird feeling about this guy.

"I have done this kind of work before, Karen, so I don't think that I will need much training," he replied.

"That's a good thing," I said as I still felt funny about being alone with him, and I couldn't wait to be in amongst others inside the room where we would be working.

This man didn't look dangerous, and if he was, what would he have to gain inside of a packing plant? I kind of laughed to myself and walked him through everything he needed to know or what I was supposed to show him before we entered the processing room.

When we were in there, everyone was focused on us. In my mind I believed that they were probably thinking the same thing that I was, and didn't really want to get to know this guy too well. I never thought about myself as being a snob, but there was something about Brian that was making me feel uncomfortable.

I spent the day explaining and showing him how to wrap meat properly, and when the day had ended and the whistle blew, letting all of us know that we could go home, I showed him where to put his gown, hat and gloves before he left the room.

In my thoughts of him having some previous training and a job doing this, I told my supervisor that I believed that he was capable of doing his job properly. I actually did believe this, and also I didn't want to be around him anymore, with him leaning toward me when he spoke, or into me when we stood next to each other. This was weird and hard to handle.

As I left the parking lot, I noticed a small car that made every turn that I did. I was on my way to Bond's Supermarket before I returned to my home. After parking my car, I glanced in my rear-view mirror. I didn't want to make it apparent that I had noticed this, as I wasn't sure if my feelings stemmed out of the unusual man that I had just finished training.

In our town of Mission last year, there was someone who had come here to rob parts and material from one of the big coal mines. We also had a business that had been set on fire, and a murder that had occurred a couple of blocks over from where I live. None of the people that had committed these acts of terror, robberies and arson had been found. I knew that the police department was still watching and trying to solve the different incidents that took place. Because of all of this, everyone living here has been very skittish of our surroundings. Especially at night, when it gets dark, and with all of us that live alone.

The car parked and no one appeared to be getting out of it. I wasn't sure if I should start my car again and leave, or take a chance and go on about my plans to enter the supermarket.

When I was young, my grandmother told me that there is no greater fear except for fear itself, so with remembering her words to me, I got out of my car and took a chance. My journey of walking and shopping in the store would be quick, but productive.

After I had been in there for a short while, I felt a hand touch my shoulder. I turned around and it was Brian. He had snuck up on me. Once again he was leaning toward me with a huge smile and bulging eyes. That night I realized that yes, I did have some fear, and seeing Brian just made it more intense. Why was he there annoying me? Was he the one in that black car, and was he planning to follow me everywhere I went? If so, *WHY?*

"I'm sorry I frightened you, Karen," Brian spoke.

"It's okay, but please don't do it again," I replied.

"Why are you so jumpy?" he asked.

"It is getting late in the day and I am in here all alone shopping. I'm sorry if I snapped at you."

"No worries, Karen. I don't have a lot of friends, and because of this I was a little nervous when I was around you at the plant today. I am sure that I have given you the wrong impression of myself. I really am a nice person," Brian said, this time with his head pointed down and no bulging eyes staring at me, or him leaning toward my face.

This was where I felt ashamed of myself for judging without really getting to know him first, before making my own judgment of his character.

"I'm sorry. You did come onto me a little stronger than what I am used to, but instead of giving you a chance,

I chose to act like a child. It won't happen again, and now that we have had this discussion, I feel as if we can be friends," I said as I smiled at him.

Brian was not only tall, but he also looked like at one time he could have been a bodyguard. He was muscular and did have a nice smile.

I said to him, "There have been a lot of things that have happened in Mission in the last year, and everyone in town is having a trust issue going on right now." Then I added with a smile, "Maybe at work it would be better to let people get to know you first, and then try to be their friend." I started making my way toward the check stand.

"Thank you, Karen, for talking to me," he replied. "I will do what you said as I don't want to scare anyone."

"That would be good. I will see you at work tomorrow. There we can talk, and with others seeing this, I don't think it will be long before you feel comfortable working there, and will be able to relax. Don't worry about everyone there liking you, as there will be those that don't, just like the ones that don't like *me*."

I had spoken from my heart and was ready to leave, wondering if the car that pulled into the parking lot was gone, or if it was maybe Brian's car. My trust issue for now had been resolved as I like to give everyone a second chance.

— 2 —

Mysteries in the Night

A s I walked out the revolving door of the store, I could still see the car that followed me parked under a big willow tree that had grown around the sidewalk beside the street. The windows of the car were dark and this car was black. There was no street light around it, and so I couldn't see if anyone was sitting in it.

In order to feed my curiosity, I sat there, waiting and watching to see if anyone from the store, being mainly Brian, came out to get into it. With everything that had taken place in Mission the last year, I needed to keep myself safe and not go over to it, looking for trouble.

Instead, I unlocked my car and sat down on the seat, swinging the grocery bags over the steering wheel to place on the passenger's side of my car. I thought about starting my car and driving away, but once again I decided to stay put for a while and watch my surroundings.

About a half hour into it, Brian came out of the store. He was carrying very little for being in the store that long, and to my surprise, he climbed into a red Corvette. This was way nicer a car than a simple meat-packing man would ever drive. It was practically new, with racing stripes.

The black car still continued to stay parked, and no one was coming out of the store to get into it. My main concern was to see if Brian was the one who had followed me, and the owner of that car, but seeing that he wasn't, I was convinced that whoever did drive it was either sitting in it, or still inside the store.

It was 10:00 p.m. with another day of work tomorrow, waiting for me in the morning, so it was time to rest my mind and go home. I started my car and left. It had to have been a coincidence for that car to have made every turn that I did and end up where I was going.

As I entered my driveway, I could see lights on in the house across the street. Apparently, the new neighbors were completely moved in. It would be an hour longer before I could lay my body down to sleep.

When I did go to bed, I wondered if I had come across too strong and hurtful toward Brian. If I had, I shouldn't have, as whatever he did at work and how he presented himself was up to him. Then again, maybe what I told him was what he needed to hear. Maybe this would give him the confidence that he needed within himself to be able to find the friends that he needed in his life.

The next day I was awakened by a running lawn mower in the new neighbor's yard. Everyone living in their home was up and ready for their day. The kids were waiting at the bus stop. It was for all the rest of us living around here a "good morning to you" and a "welcome to the neighborhood" kind of day. These were my thoughts as I giggled to myself.

I lay in bed for a while longer and then it was time to wake up. It was going to be an interesting day. Putting on my bathrobe and slippers, I went down my stairs to get coffee and sit in the living room, watching the morning news, before returning to the bedroom to finish getting ready for my day.

As I sat down on the couch, I heard a news report that really hit home. The report was about the supermarket that Brian and I were in last night. Sometime during the night, an explosion had done a lot of damage. This was nothing that I wanted or needed to hear. It was yet another incident taking place in the town of Mission. No one had been hurt or killed. Things had reached a point to where everyone in town was leery of going anywhere, not knowing what to expect.

After getting to work, I would find out if anyone else had heard the news report.

It was time to finish getting ready. I turned off the television and went back upstairs. Soon after, I grabbed my keys that I had set on my night stand, and walked down the stairs to leave my home.

As I drove past the new neighbor's home, he was still on the riding lawn mower. He nodded and waved at me as I did him. From what I could see, they looked like nice people whom I hoped liked living here.

That morning it appeared as if everyone who worked at the plant had gotten there at the same time. Brian had arrived in his expensive Corvette, which was so nice that it made every one of us workers' cars stand out like something we all bought from a salvage yard. Once again I was giggling to myself. I guess I was wondering with the jobs that he had listed on his résumé of work that he had done in the past, how could he afford a really nice car like this?

After everyone in the plant was where they needed to be, Brian waved at me from across the room. He pointed at the exit of the meat-packing room, and so I shook my head yes and put up ten fingers. I was telling him that at 10 o'clock, when we had our coffee break, we could talk then. He shook his head yes, which meant he understood.

When the whistle blew, all of us filed out to take a break. We all took our gloves, hats and gowns off before leaving and followed the crowd to the coffee machine. Soon Brian joined me, and we were ready to talk.

"Brian, did you hear the news this morning?" I asked.

"No, Karen, I didn't. Was there something on it that I should know about?" he asked.

"They were saying that an explosion went off at the supermarket last night, where you and I were at. When I was in there, I didn't see anything strange going on. Did you?" I asked.

"No. I just got what I needed and left the store like everyone else. Did they catch the person or people responsible for this?"

"Not that I am aware of. I did notice you when you left. It didn't look like you were carrying much," I said.

"I wasn't. I am not a big eater and it was late. Now that this has happened, where do we go for groceries?" he asked.

"There is a market not far from there. It isn't large, but it's big enough."

We had taken our turns getting coffee and went to sit down on the chairs.

"Have you lived here your whole life?" I asked.

"No, I just came to Mission last week. I originated from Washington, D.C. I lived in Salt Lake City for a while before I moved here," Brian answered.

"Wow, you have already had quite a life. What did you do in Washington, D.C.?" I asked.

"Let's just say that I had a much better job," he said, laughing.

I guess that explained the nice red Corvette with racing stripes that he drove. He must have had money tucked away somewhere to buy it.

The whistle blew and the coffee break was over. It was again time to wash our hands and get ready to go back to our jobs.

Brian said we would talk again and I was sure that we would. There was still a mysterious side to him that I wanted to find out about.

The day progressed and again the whistle blew for us to quit for the day. When all of us left the room, we put our caps, gloves and gowns in the baskets that were furnished.

I noticed Brian talking to another man who worked there. It appeared that he was making friends and this was not only good for him, but also good for me as well. Brian was a nice guy after all, but with all of the doubts in my mind about him, from the first moment that I had seen him, at the time I wasn't ready to be on his list of being his buddy.

This time, instead of making a detour to a store, I just went home. I wanted to listen to more news about the explosion. After unlocking the door to my house and setting the keys on the counter, I shut and locked the door to return once again to the television. Just as I turned it on, I heard, "We have a news announcement for all of you in Mission, Utah. Once again someone has caused destruction. This time it was in Bond's Supermarket. No one is allowed in or around the building as there is an investigation going on. A couple of people have stepped forward to give what information they have to the police department. Not wanting to be seen on television, we are not allowed to disclose their names or faces. The only information that we have for you is that apparently one of the cars spotted at the store before this happened was a black car with tinted windows. This car is a 2000 Mercury Town Car. If you see anything suspicious happening, or any black car that fits this description that may have been involved, please contact the police department in Mission, Utah, immediately. Another car was seen driving away as well, but we have no description on it as of yet. This has been a local broadcast."

With this information, I was even more convinced that I had seen the same black car that they were referring to. It had to have been the one parked across the street behind me in the parking area of Bond's.

The rest of the evening with this on my mind, I sat at my kitchen table, eating very little and still listening for more updates on the news. After several hours, I decided to let it go in my wanting to get all the facts presented to everyone watching the broadcast, and again just go to bed.

Being somewhat nervous, my anxiety kicked in. The next thing that I did was make sure that all the windows and doors were locked.

In the morning, I woke up later than I should have

and was busy rushing around to get ready for work. Before I walked out the side door, I grabbed a donut and a cup of coffee.

As I was driving to work, three fire trucks passed me at a high rate of speed. I could see smoke in the air coming from a distance. It was hard to tell if it was coming from a burning building or something else. Because of all the disasters that had and were occurring, all I could hope for was that there wasn't another one taking place at this moment.

Before I got to the interstate exit that would take me to the packing plant, five police cars went zooming past me as well. Whatever this was had to be something big.

When I finally did exit off the interstate, I could see that there were many of my co-workers who had just arrived. Wondering if they knew anything, because I had missed watching the news that morning, I walked up to Cheryl, who also worked in packaging meat, and asked, "Did you see all the fire trucks and police cars?"

"Yes, this is why I am getting here now, and hopefully I'm not late. There was another explosion this morning, just before I left home ... this time in the courthouse building. This makes *two* explosions in a couple of days," Cheryl replied.

"Not another one! I hope they catch who is doing this. Do they have any leads on who it is?" I asked.

"I don't think so, other than the same black car driving away from the building in the morning that was spotted by a man who was outside early, walking his dog."

"Mission has turned into a scary place to live. The sad part is that this has been going on for a year now, and I would think that by now our police department would have a lead on who is doing all of the destruction," I said as Cheryl and I entered the plant.

She went her way to prepare for her job, and I went my way. I looked around and there was no sign of Brian. Being so busy talking to Cheryl outside, I didn't think to look at the parking lot to see if his red car was there. Maybe he had chosen not to work here any longer, or maybe he was late because of the backed-up traffic that had to let all the emergency vehicles through.

An hour went by and then I saw Brian enter the room. He was late. He waved at me and then went straight to the table to start preparing and wrapping the meat.

When the whistle blew at 10:00, once again he pointed at the door. I nodded my head yes and left the table to get coffee and talk to him for a while. Maybe he had something important that he wanted to tell me.

"Karen, I see that you made it to work on time," Brian said.

"Yes, but just barely. Were you caught in the traffic jam?" I asked.

"No, I was somewhere else. I had business that I had to take care of."

"When I got here, there were those of us who were just making it to work," I told him. "A co-worker told me that there was another explosion—at the courthouse. There was a black car again, spotted by a man walking his dog. Mission was a calm place to live until this and other things started happening. Now, for some reason, the police department is having trouble finding the person or persons involved in this. Many lives have been at risk," I commented.

"I am sure that before long, Karen, this will stop around here," Brian said, looking very confident in what he had just said.

"I can only hope so, Brian," I replied as the whistle blew and once again we were all on our way back to our different stations where we worked in the plant.

The rest of the day once again went fairly quickly, and it was time for all of us to clear out of the building and go home. Tomorrow was Saturday and no work for any of us. This would be the day when I had to make my way downtown to shop and also take care of my own business.

The interstate was back to normal, and within minutes I was pulling into my driveway.

The neighbor across the street waved again when I drove past. He was outside watching his children play ball in the street. I wondered if he watched the news, and if so, how long he and his family would be staying here.

After I unlocked the door to my home, I was ready again to see if the local news had something on it about the explosion that had taken place that day. For some odd reason, there was nothing being said about it. This was unusual as this explosion didn't just happen in a store or business, it had happened in a government building. To me this was a big deal.

I warmed up a dinner in the microwave and sat down to continue to listen and see if later on in the news, the broadcasters would show a report or talk about what had happened.

I sat there for hours and nothing was being said, so I turned off the television and went to bed. I was tired from my day and was planning on being able to drift off to sleep. This was easier said than done, as after I got comfortable, I heard more fire trucks and police cars ripping down the interstate. Something *else* was happening. This time, instead of jumping out of bed to see if I could find out anything, I couldn't stay awake and went to sleep.

In the morning, when I woke up and walked downstairs in my bathrobe and slippers, I went to the coffee pot to get a cup of coffee. Then I sat down on the couch to watch the news, in hopes of the television broadcaster showing or telling something.

Again on the local news, no one said anything. This now was making me wonder why. I went to the phone and called the television station. The phone rang twice and then a man answered the phone.

"KKRV," he said.

"Yes, this is Karen Albertson, and I have a simple question to ask you. Is there a reason why the explosions that are still taking place in Mission, Utah, aren't being broadcast?" I asked.

"Yes, Karen. The FBI is involved now, and they have asked us not to broadcast anything else about the destruction that is being done there. I am sorry I can't help you."

At that moment, there was nothing more for me to say except, "Wow!"

Again the man apologized for not being able to help me, and I told him that I understood and that I was happy that the FBI had been called in to help solve the problem.

Knowing this now, the only thing left to do was sit back and wait to see what the FBI uncovered. With me thinking this, it made me wonder why Brian had said that it would all stop around here soon. Did he know something that he wasn't telling me?

It was getting late and I needed to get ready for my day. It was "up and at it" for me.

As I drove into town, the traffic on the interstate was back to normal. No traffic jams, fire trucks or police cars. When I drove into the parking area of the market, I saw Brian coming out of the store. He saw me and waved. After parking and turning off my car, I rolled my window down. Brian was walking toward me.

"Good morning, Karen. You are out early today."

"I have things that I need to do and wanted to beat the rush hour traffic," I replied.

"I have been up and out of my apartment for hours now. The other day at the supermarket I failed to grab some things that I needed, so this was on my list of what I needed to get done today, as apparently it was on yours as well."

"Did you see the smoke in the air and hear the fire trucks last night?" I asked.

"Yes, I did," he replied.

"Do you know anything about what happened?" I asked.

"At the moment, it is being taken care of," he said.

"Okay, that is good," I replied as I stepped out of my car.

"I will talk to you later," Brian said as he started walking away.

I waved at him and kept walking, wondering why he was in a hurry and acted like what had happened during the night was not really of significance. Also, why had he said that it was being *taken care of now?* My curiosity was getting out of control and this time it was again focused on Brian. He appeared okay, but I felt even more like there was more to this man than just being a co-worker at the plant. He was always on the go and seemed to have an insight into things that I couldn't find out about. Who was this man? The truth was that none of us knew in Mission.

After getting enough food for a few days, I returned to my car to go farther into town to a shop where I needed to be at, to pick up some things that I had taken in to be altered. My cousin was getting married in a few weeks and that would mean a trip back to Mesquite for the wedding. Maybe this was exactly what I needed.

As I was driving slowly in town, I glanced over as I saw Brian standing around, talking to a man wearing an expensive suit. The man had a paper in his hand and was showing Brian something on it. Whatever it was could have been anything, but I could see that with the look on both of their faces, they were really concentrating on something.

Not far from there was a black car with tinted windows. Now wheels were really turning in my head, and I was probably imagining things that weren't there. There was more than one black car in town, and it might have belonged to a worker who was standing around, removing rubble from a construction site in that area.

I kept driving and taking care of all the errands that I needed to do. On my way back home, I took the same route from town as I took going into town. When I passed the area where I had seen Brian talking to one man, this time I saw him standing around, talking to five men. They were all wearing nice suits. I knew that something was being said, as I could see it in their expressions. Brian had told me that he was more or less a loner, and didn't have any friends. This now seemed strange to me. Was he lying? What were they doing there?

Not wanting to consume myself with something that wasn't my business, I kept driving.

When I returned home, I saw a sheriff's car sitting across the street at my new neighbor's house. After I had gone inside, I continued to watch them for a while. They were looking at a big picture window that looked like it had been broken from maybe a passing driver on our street. Seeing this gave me thoughts of whether or not havoc was also going to start in neighborhoods now as well as the destruction that had been caused in stores and the courthouse. Whatever the case may be, I was wondering if maybe my new neighbors might be sorry they had moved to this neighborhood.

I shut the curtain and did what I wanted and needed to do for the rest of the day. After a while, my phone rang and I could see that it was my dad calling. "Hello, Dad," I said as I answered the phone.

"Hello, Karen."

"It's good to hear your voice again. How are you and Mom?"

"We are doing good, Karen. I am calling in regards to you. Your mother and I have been keeping up with your local news for some time now. It appears that there is more activity going on in Mission than should be," Dad replied.

"Yes, there is a bunch now, Dad, and from what I have been told, the FBI is involved and hopefully it won't be long now until the man or men are caught."

"Just watch your surroundings, Karen. Be aware of everyone that you meet or are approached by," Dad commented.

"I am, Dad. Don't worry as I am being careful."

"Okay, Karen, keep me updated."

"I will," I replied.

Our conversation was short and I was surprised that our local news had spread all the way to Mesquite.

I had finished what I needed to do in the house and walked over to sit on the couch, to once again listen to the news. My mind kept drifting back to Brian, wondering what he was doing or what he was up to. Could he be the one that the FBI was looking for that was involved in some way with all of this? He was new in Mission, according to him, strange in manner and very mysterious. In reality's sake, I really didn't know anything about him. He was late getting to work, and spending a bunch of time talking to many men wearing suits. He had informed me that he'd had business to take care of before he had arrived at the plant. My inner self was telling me that I needed to be careful what I said to him and to make sure that I was safe at all times.

I got up from the couch and made my way upstairs for the evening. I had to find a way not to consume my thoughts on something that I couldn't control, or change. This time, when I lay down to sleep, I heard no noise from fire trucks or police cars zooming past on the interstate. The night was silent and peaceful for a change.

When morning came, I woke up to the noise that I had expected to hear during the night. There was a lot of smoke in the air. Knowing that the television station wasn't going to broadcast anything about what was taking place, I decided that I was going to make today a good day without worries or concentrating on anything bad. I had a baby shower to attend in the afternoon for a co-worker. What I didn't know was that Brian was again talking to the same men that I had seen him with yesterday.

"So what do you think?" a short, round man wearing a dark grey suit asked.

"I know we are on the right track," Brian replied with

a confident look.

"Is anyone at the place where you work curious about you?" asked another man, who was dressed in a long-sleeved dress shirt with a nice pair of brown slacks and a light tan vest.

"No one suspects anything. As far as they know, I am just another worker going there each day, putting in my time to collect a paycheck at the end of the week. I am onto something, though, and we will see how it turns out," Brian spoke.

"You need to be careful as now is not the time for us to be known to anyone," said another man, wearing a black suit with a dark blue tie, as he had overheard the conversation of Brian and the other men as he approached them.

"Right now, we have business to handle, and at the plant I am just keeping it short, sweet and believable," Brian replied.

During this time of Brian's conversation, I had already left for the drive to my co-worker's home. When I exited off of the interstate onto a street that would take me where I needed to be, I saw a black Town Car, and to my amazement, Brian's red Corvette was behind it. This was a coincidence like none other, and when I passed him, he waved at me. I kept on driving and thought that it was a good day and I had no time for nonsense going through my mind.

When the day was finished and I had once again returned home, watched the news, and relaxed from all the excitement of the afternoon, it was time to go to bed and be prepared for another week of work.

The next morning, when all of us were working hard at our jobs, Brian walked through the door two hours late. When he noticed me, he once again waved at me. I couldn't believe that he was showing up late again today. The traffic was smooth this morning and back to normal. I knew that if things continued the way they were, he wouldn't have a job at the plant much longer.

After a few hours, the whistle blew, telling us that it was once again break time. As I was standing in line, waiting my turn to get something to drink, Brian approached me.

"Brian, you are getting good at being late for work," I said.

"I know. I had business that I needed to take care of again that was important," he replied.

"Did you read the handbook that came with this job?" I asked. "Can't you take care of it after work?"

"Yes, I read the handbook. Sometimes I can do that."

"Aren't you worried about losing your job that you just started?"

"Not really," Brian replied with an expression on his face as if he wanted us to keep our conversation simple, without a lot of questions. So from now on, this was what I was going to do.

When the whistle blew, we were all filing back to our jobs.

— 3 —

Should I or Shouldn't I?

A t quitting time, when all of the other workers had left the plant to go home, I decided that I was going to do my best to follow Brian, to see just what kind of business he was taking care of. There were so many things about this man that intrigued me. How could a man who drove a nice, almost new, red Corvette not care about his job? In Mission, good jobs weren't a dime a dozen. It took years of working at the plant in order to even start to qualify for a job worthy enough to be able to buy a car like that. Then there was the cost of maintaining it, along with rent or mortgage, food, gas, utilities, et cetera.

When he had left the parking lot, I pulled out shortly after. I didn't want him to know that I was tailing him. It wasn't right what I was doing, but I had a funny feeling about his after-hours activities that he had been doing. Brian was a nice, friendly man, or at least appeared to be. Then again, many convicted men were friendly, but still criminals. At work I was going to loosen up on him. It was irritating him as he didn't like having to explain himself. For all I knew, he might be the one behind the horrible acts that had and were taking place in Mission. I was pretty sure that he knew more than he wanted me to be aware of.

I continued to stay several car links behind him. When he made a turn, I made the same turn in hopes that he didn't see me. Here I was, a young woman with no detective capabilities, or knowledge on how it was done, sticking my neck out for our town and our well being. Again while driving, I had to laugh at myself. What excuse would I use if he saw me and asked me about why I was following him?

A light turned red, and so I was stopped for a while. When the light turned green, I continued driving in the direction I was going, thinking that there was that chance that I had lost Brian's car, that he had turned off the street we were on.

After a while, I saw his car parked at the same spot downtown, where I had seen him talking to the men wearing suits. There was no place for me to park except beside his car. If I parked there and got out of my car, it wasn't like I could just walk up on all of them and listen to their conversation. So now that I had myself in this predicament, it would mean that I would be driving past him and he would see me. I was going to need to come up with a really good story in order to throw him off track of what he might believe I was doing. Unfortunately, he would be right.

I slowly passed, pretending to be surprised to see him standing there. He waved at me and I smiled and waved back. I had created a real mess for myself, and before tomorrow I knew that I should come up with some kind of explanation why I was in that part of town. Even though I could go anywhere in Mission that I wanted to, and didn't need to justify my actions to him or to anyone else, I again chuckled and realized that I wasn't cut out to be a detective and that now I knew why detectives made the big bucks.

Since I was already downtown, I decided to eat out at a restaurant close by. As I sat there, looking around the room and waiting for the waitress, to my surprise I saw Brian coming through the door. He wasn't where I had just seen him for very long. This time he didn't see me as I was hidden in a corner of the room.

There were a couple of men, again with suits on, sitting at a table not far from the front door. Brian went over to them and sat down. The waitress was already there, taking orders from each one of them. I could see their mouths moving, but I couldn't hear what was being said.

Brian had ordered just coffee, and the other men had ordered off the menu. My guess was that he wasn't going to be sitting there that long. At their table they continued to talk.

"This is going faster than we thought it would," Brian said.

"We know, and all of us are ready whenever you give the okay," a man said, hardly moving his mouth.

"Do you think anyone knows who we are?" a different man asked.

"No one is the wiser. It won't be much longer," Brian replied to them.

Even if I could have read lips, I would have struggled to read any of theirs.

I saw that Brian was ready to get up from his chair, and not having a clue what he had said, I turned and dropped my napkin on the floor. Then I bent over to pick it up, watching out of the corner of my eye to see when Brian was out of view. Brian might have seen me, but my guess was that he hadn't.

I was completely done playing detective that day and sat there, casually eating my meal. By the time I finished, the two men got up and left. Where they went after the restaurant was not known to me. I paid for my meal and left to walk out to where I had parked my car.

On the drive back home, it was dark. I realized that detective work was not for me as it was somewhat scary. I could have gotten shot, and from now on, I was leaving all of this up to the actual FBI.

As for Brian, there would be no more questions as, if I was right about him, this would make me a target.

The rest of the week at the plant, I spoke to Brian, but kind of left him alone as well. I was sure that he probably wondered why, but I had run out of things to talk to him about. He continued to show up late for work and left in the same direction, taking him into town every day.

It was Friday night and I had to go back into town to shop. My plans for the weekend were going to take me out of town to a cabin that I had rented. I needed the rest, to get away from Mission and all the sirens, fire trucks and police cars—and also the wonderment about how I could have been fooled by what I thought was a nice man like Brian.

I drove into town, not caring if I saw him, and if I did, I wasn't going to wave or smile this time, if I saw that he was with the small group of other men.

When I reached the same spot where they always stood, I saw none of them. In a way, I was relieved, but then again I began to wonder if they were all at a certain area, and if they were planning more destructive in Mission.

That afternoon I had to go farther into town, which meant going over an overpass that was well traveled. This was not on my list of favorite things to do as the overpass was lengthy and slippery. It had stormed that day and the snow was still falling from the sky.

When I started up the overpass, my car started making a noise like I hadn't heard before. Every time I stepped on the gas, it acted like it wanted to stop running. I was sure it probably wasn't anything that would ruin my weekend plans, but decided to pull off the interstate, catch a ride home, and call a mechanic to fix it.

I got out of my car and went to the passenger side to put my thumb out to show people driving past that I needed help. When I turned my head, I saw what appeared to be two men standing under the overpass. This was great as I thought they would give me the ride that I needed to go home.

My being a small town woman that walked softly, the two men were busy doing something and didn't hear me when I walked toward them. I could see their arms stretching up, but thought maybe they were hired to work on the overpass, so I continued to walk in their direction.

As I arrived where they were standing, I could see that I was in the wrong spot at the wrong time. They were both stuffing dynamite into the bottom of the overpass. My guess was that they were going to blow it up as cars were driving on it.

I turned around to walk away and run, but just then one of the men saw me. He ran after me and grabbed me from behind. He then dragged me back to where I couldn't be seen by anyone driving by.

"You shouldn't have come over here," he said.

"Please let me go. I am not a threat to you," I cried out.

"You know that isn't going to happen," he said.

"Why are you doing this to all of us?" I asked.

"That is none of your business!" he yelled at me.

By then I felt so much fear that all I could do was stand there, screaming and crying.

"SHUT UP!" the man said as the other man continued to stuff dynamite under the overpass.

I was still being jerked around, and the man that had hold of me tied me to a steep pole that was there. He then took tape that they had and wrapped it around my face, covering my mouth. I was sure that I had no chance of survival, and according to the man who tied me up, my time spent that day would be my last. I couldn't move and was sure that what he had said was right.

The two men continued to stuff the overpass, and I noticed that Brian and the men that he had been hanging out with were slowly creeping up on them. They all had guns pointed at the creeps that wanted to destroy us all.

When Brian shoved a gun into one of the men's backs, another man wearing a suit did the same to the other guy. Then I heard what they said.

"You are under arrest. Put your hands behind your

back and don't even think about running away. We are the FBI and you are in a lot of trouble."

The two men knew they had been caught and that there was nothing either one of them could do. Two of the FBI men grabbed them and handcuffed them, then took them in the direction they had come from, to put them in the back of their car. The other two men stood there, digging out the dynamite from under the overpass.

Brian walked over to me. "Karen, I am sure that you have a bunch of questions for me today. I will make sure that you get home safely as I saw your car sitting off the interstate. Then later, I will come by your home and explain things to you," he said. Then Brian untied me and unwrapped the tape from my head and mouth.

"I am so happy that you are here. I was afraid," I said as I burst into tears.

"I know, and there is nothing to fear now, Karen," said Brian as he took out his handkerchief to wipe away some tears from my eyes.

He then instructed the last man standing there in a suit to take me home.

Later in the day, when Brian was finished at the police department, he came to my home to talk to me. I heard a knock and knew it was him.

"Come in, Brian," I said.

"Thank you, Karen. Actually, my name isn't Brian Osborn. It is David Marono. I changed my identity when I came to town. I am a well known FBI agent, and we couldn't take a chance that I would be recognized by my real name. This was too big of an operation. I am sorry to deceive you like that, but it was critical that I did."

Then he said, "A few weeks ago, your dad called me on the phone. I have known him for years. I met him when I first started working for the FBI. At that time, he was retired from the Secret Service, but when he was needed, he still continued to work for them undercover.

"Your dad knew that the police department was

doing their best to solve all of this, but they needed some help. He was also very worried about you, and today was a prime example of what could have happened to you if we didn't get there in time.

"He told me where you worked and asked me to keep an eye on you. I told him that I would. The man that manages the plant has known all along who I am, and when we contacted him, he was sworn to silence. That is why I could get by with showing up late for work each day. I carried a fake ID to protect myself as well from the truth coming out as this was of major importance for all of you in Mission, and for this operation to be carried out and handled the right way.

"It wasn't a coincidence why you were the one that was asked to train me for my job. I requested that you be the one to do this, and that I be placed in the same area where you were working. This way I could get to know you, and be there to protect you.

"I acted the way I did with the bulging eyes and leaning toward you for a reason. I had to make myself look weird so that everyone in the plant would just look at me as being odd and unusual, and they would leave me alone, in order for me to investigate all of them without drawing attention to myself.

"I knew that you were starting to doubt my character and was somewhat curious about where I went each day after work. Karen, I knew that you were following me, and during that time I saw you in my car as I drove, I had to laugh, knowing that you were playing detective.

"What you didn't know was that at times when you didn't see me, I was watching *you* as well. I had promised your dad that I would keep you safe, and no matter what, I was going to do just that.

"We had also become friends and, at times, I did want you to think the worst of me. This is why on coffee breaks I pretended to be stupid about certain things, because all of us agents were getting close to finding out who had been causing all of the destruction around here. The investigations had been going on by the police here, but they needed us to help them out this time. I had to pretend to be just one of your co-workers that was new to town.

"I know that you were wondering how an underpaid employee who had worked at minimal jobs could afford a nice car such as mine. Now you know as I work for the federal government. I have been doing this for many years and, yes, I did go to school in Washington, D.C. This is also where I got my training. I have worked my way up the ladder to the top. It is hard work, but I enjoy it as I have been a part of helping many people.

"Now my question to you is, can you forgive me for deceiving you?" David asked as he continued to stand in my living room, smiling at me.

"Yes, David, I can forgive you," I said. "I am so happy that finally this mystery is solved. I don't care if your name is Brian or David. You saved my life and many more lives today. I am proud to call you my friend. I knew that my dad worked for the Secret Service, but I didn't put the connection together when I heard that the FBI had taken over the case."

"Your dad is very good at his job. He was very worried about you and your town. He wanted everyone here to feel at peace again. He also knew that he could count on me for anything and that I wouldn't let him down."

"Now what are your plans?" I asked.

"We will all return to Washington, D.C., Karen. If you like, I will keep in contact with you," David said.

"Yes, I would like that. I have to say, though, that I will miss seeing you at the plant," I said with a slight giggle.

"I know, Karen. I will miss your smile as well. You were willing to give me a chance at the plant when others there didn't. That means a lot to me. I will call you from time to time, and we can talk about how you are doing, and when I can, I will update you on myself with what information I can give out that isn't going to interfere with my job."

"That would be great," I said as David shook my hand gently and walked toward the door.

"Take care of yourself," he said as he opened the door and walked away to get into his car.

As David drove away, he waved at me. Would this be our last time that we spent together? At that moment, I thought that only time would tell.

Over the weeks to come, we talked a lot on the phone. I looked forward to coming home at night because I knew David would be calling me. Our friendship had gone from my thinking I was training an unusual man that annoyed me for a job in the meat-packing plant to a man whom I couldn't trust, as in my mind I kept wondering, "Is he or isn't he the one the FBI and police department are looking for?" I had no way of knowing, in reality, that this man was brave and an FBI agent who was handling the case.

When it came time for my cousin's wedding, I called David and he drove out to be with me at the wedding. My dad was very happy to see us together and he shook David's hand again.

After the wedding, David and I spent a bunch of time together and were becoming closer than just friends. My thoughts had changed from "is he or isn't he the crook?" to "is he or isn't he the man of my dreams?"

Within a year, I gave up my job at the meat packing plant and moved to Washington, D.C. I started a new career, and after another year of seeing David, we married in my home town of Mesquite. It always amazes me when I look back on all of what took place in Mission, how two people who were so different could find each other.

Sometimes the least person that you believe will be your soul mate turns out to be the one person that you don't ever want to live without.

THE UNEXPLAINABLE

PART 5

CHECK IN,
BUT CAN'T CHECK OUT

— 1 —

Preparation and More

In a small town in West Virginia, two young women are talking on the phone, discussing a road trip that they are anxious and excited about.

They had been planning this getaway for several years and knew that the day was finally here. They are ready for an adventure of their lifetime.

With them having the route that they are taking mapped out, their schedule of what would take place each day was already on paper.

These young women had just graduated from separate universities. They had been best friends since grade school and decided years ago that there would come a day when they would make this trip a reality.

They were leaving their hometown of Bailey to explore, view and experience all the beauty from Bailey, West Virginia to Long Beach, California.

My name is Patty Morris, or as everyone calls me, Pat. I am one of the girls that I am talking about. My life-long friend Diane Gibbs is the other girl who will be taking this journey with me.

As I said, we are fresh out of college and we worked hard to not only pay our tuition, but also to save money for this adventure. Of course, our parents thought that we shouldn't go, and Diane and I expected this. It was going to be a long road trip with lots of camping and motel stops waiting for us.

Neither one of us were fresh out of high school and fairly sure that we could handle this trip without parental supervision. We started preparing for this trip after graduation in May. As I sat in the bleachers with Diane's family, cheering her on when she was handed her diploma, she was sitting and waiting with my family, watching me receive mine.

When we announced to both sets of parents that we were taking this long trip, the first thing they said was, "You are two silly girls that think just because you graduated from college, you can do anything, no matter how dangerous it is."

Maybe? But in spite of the negative beliefs and remarks, we were doing it anyway.

The next step to our plan was to get everything that we would need. The first thing we got were sleeping bags. This was a necessity, for if we got tired from driving and didn't want to continue on with our travels that day, we could always stop and build a campfire and sleep outdoors. Coming from a small town, we were fearless at the time, and nothing was going to stop us. Not even a bear that might wander onto us.

That day shopping, we not only bought sleeping bags, but also coolers, gallons of water, a fire starter, charcoal and flashlights.

Our thoughts were that if we needed anything else, we could always stop along the way and pick it up.

My dad, against his wishes but not wanting us to take the chance of something bad happening to us, took my car to a shop to get new tires and also a tune-up.

We had packed our clothes, had extra blankets, a car jack—just in case we did get a flat tire—and we already had food inside the cooler.

The next and final thing to do was say goodbye to our parents, who stood on the curb, looking as if they would never see us again. I started my car and pulled away as we waved at them.

It wasn't long and we were on an interstate going west. We had mapped out routes that would take us to scenic places that, for the last six years, we had only dreamed about. In Kentucky, we wanted to visit the Louisville Mega Cavern. It was a limestone mine. Also, we were going to find a place to bike in the mountains.

In Arkansas, we wanted to visit the Blanchard Spring Caverns. There were caves in the Ozark-St. Francis Forest off of the highway. We had been told that it was called the Half Mile Cave.

Next on the list was the State Fair and Rodeo in Texas. We wanted to drive on the Bluebonnet Trail, canoe or boat, and next would be the Inner Space Cavern, to see prehistoric remains. We were looking forward to Blue Bell ice cream, a Texas barbecue, and the Buddy Holly Museum. In Arizona there was the Grand Canyon, Cathedral Rock and red rock formations.

At last, when we had reached our destination of Long Beach, California, we were extremely excited about riding the Catalina Express to the beautiful island of Catalina in the Pacific Ocean. We had heard that it was like living in Paradise on Earth, and of course the huge attraction of the *Queen Mary*.

This was our itinerary, but as you know, sometimes things have a way of changing.

By the time it started getting dark, we had reached our first stop. We had left the interstate and had been driving on a country road for some time. No motel was in sight, so our first night would be spent in the great outdoors with our sleeping bags.

"Pat, I don't know about you, but I have had fun today," Diane commented. "The air smells so clean and fresh."

"I know. Isn't it beautiful here? We have waited a long time to take this adventure," I responded.

"Yes, and it is all going to be worth the wait," Diane replied.

"I don't think we are going to need the fire starter tonight, and we can sleep in our sleeping bags, looking at the moon and stars until we go to sleep. In the morning, I will build a campfire and we can eat breakfast before we leave," I said.

Diane agreed, and we walked to the car to get the sleeping bags out of the back seat. After we had unrolled them onto the ground, we lay inside of them, looking up at the beautiful sky.

We had been there for about fifteen minutes, and then we heard a rustle in the bushes close by.

"What was that?" Diane asked as she sat up abruptly in her sleeping bag.

"I don't know, but the wind isn't blowing," I replied.

"If it is all right with you, Pat, I am sleeping in your car," Diane spoke as she climbed out of her sleeping bag and ran to the car.

"I'm not staying out here by myself!" I said as I followed her, running as well.

After we climbed inside of it, with Diane in the back seat and me in the front, I locked the doors. Whatever was out there would need to come through my car to get to us.

As we lay there with one blanket each for us to keep warm, we started laughing. This was our first night of camping in the wilderness, and our sleeping bags were outside on the ground and we were inside my car with one blanket apiece. For every action there is a reaction, and at that time our reaction wasn't the best choice.

We were behaving like we were born and raised in the city. We continued to giggle and decided that this part of our trip we would leave out of our conversations when telling anyone about our "roughing it" in the great outdoors.

The next morning we woke up to sore backs and necks from the uncomfortable night of sleep. As both of us sat up and climbed out of my car, we were twisting, turning and rubbing our necks in hopes of undoing the kinks that we had.

"Diane, if it is okay with you, I would like to wait on the campfire breakfast," I said.

"That works for me, Pat," Diane replied.

We picked our sleeping bags up off the ground, still feeling stupid for leaving them there, and put them into the back seat. As we drove away, we agreed that in the nights that would follow, we would build a campfire and this would chase away anything and everything that could harm us as we slept.

This sounded good, but in her mind and mine, I knew we were both doubting it.

When the sun was even brighter, we passed the "Welcome to Kentucky" sign. We had come this far, and were headed in the right direction to our first scenic wonder. There was so much beauty that surrounded us, and we were again excited for our adventure that we had chosen to take.

"Pat, let's stop for a while in the next town. We can get gas, eat, and stretch our legs."

"We can do that. There might be something of interest there," I replied.

"Let's check out the river park!" Diane said as she watched a man and woman who were rafting.

We had walked over to a small bridge and stood there for a while, looking at not just rafters but also men dressed in wetsuits, canoeing down the river. From there we followed a small trail that circled and took us back to where we first started our hike.

It was time for us to leave, and once more we were driving west.

— 2 —

Wonders and Beauty

The second night when we stopped to sleep, we had found a roadside camping area where other people had also stopped to rest. This was the perfect spot to stop. We were happy that this night we weren't going to be alone in the wilderness.

"Pat, there is a tour bus," Diane spoke as she pointed to a big bus that had the words THE SHAKERS written on it.

People who had stopped there were gathered around it as four men stood, singing and playing their instruments. One of the men continued to sing, but kept looking at me.

"I think that guy likes you, Pat," Diane said and smiled.

"I doubt it. He just picked me out of the crowd here to sing to. This probably helps him with the songs," I responded.

Just before it got dark, the men stopped entertaining us and the young man walked over to us. "Sorry to stare at you. You remind me of a girl that I haven't seen in years."

Even though at that time I was thinking and wanting to say, "*That* is a familiar pick-up line," I didn't, and instead said, "It's okay. You didn't offend me by doing that."

"My name is Shawn Taylor," he said as he put his hand out to shake mine.

"Hi. I'm Patty Morris, and my friend is Diane Gibbs."

"It's nice to meet both of you," Shawn replied.

"I like your band," said Diane.

"Thank you. We have been traveling across country for several months now, performing in difference places."

"I can see why, as you do draw a crowd of people," I responded.

"Where are you from?" asked Shawn.

"We come from Bailey, West Virginia. We are on a road trip as well," I replied.

"You come from a nice area. My band and I performed in a town not far from there a few months ago."

"We have been planning our trip for several years. "We just graduated from different universities."

"I, too, am a college graduate. I went to Yale. My family expected me to start working right away. I did apply at many law firms, but after a while I got tired of waiting around for a reply back. My old band from high school was making money, traveling around, and asked me to join them. So here I am," Shawn said.

By then, another guy from the band had noticed Diane and was walking over to talk to her. "My name is Sam Roberts," he told Diane.

"Nice to meet you. I'm Diane Gibbs."

"Where are you headed?" Sam asked.

"We are on our way to California," Diane responded as she sat down next to Sam on a park bench.

Shawn and I continued to talk as Sam and Diane did. Soon after, Sam told us that they had to leave and help load the bus. We told them goodbye and good luck with all the performances that they had planned, and then walked away to return to my car, to once again try our best at camping out under the stars. This time, like all the other campers, we had built a campfire.

It wasn't long after that and we were asleep. Having others around, camping with their families, helped. I guess the child side of us felt protected.

175

In the morning, when we were up, there were many campers loading their vehicles or cooking breakfast on an open campfire. The tour bus was gone. Diane and I had enjoyed being entertained by all the musicians. We were convinced that someday maybe our paths would cross again.

Like the previous morning, we opted out on cooking outside. We didn't have a long drive until we would be at our first scenic spot that we had waited to see, this being the Louisville Mega Cavern.

After showering in the bath house and buying a cup of coffee from the manager of the park, we rolled up our sleeping bags and placed them in my car. We were on our way.

As we continued to drive, we told stories of all the fun we had together from grade school all the way up till now. We had been through not only disappointments in our lives, but also had experienced a ton of joy.

We made an exit off the highway and parked in the area provided for the tour of the cavern. It was a limestone mine under Watterson Expressway, and zoo. Because of all the support structures, it was like a building, and the largest one in the state of Kentucky. We took a tram guided tour underground. We were told that during the war it was used as a fallout shelter. When the tour was finished, it was just as amazing as we had pictured it to be. This was something that we would never forget.

Before we left, we asked the tour guide if there was another bike park close by, where we could go to. He told us about a place that rented bikes and said that if we went there, we would enjoy our ride.

We found a small cabin to rent for the night that would accommodate us. There we prepared a great meal of steaks, mashed potatoes and a can of kidney beans. The cabins were furnished with lots of pots and pans. We had bought a slice of chocolate cake, and this would be our dessert. This being the first good meal that we had eaten since we left Bailey, it was a feast to us.

Because of all the excitement and fun of the day, we were tired, but we were talking for a while until we closed our eyes to rest.

In the morning, we woke up later than we had planned. The country air was cool and refreshing, unlike the pollution from the factories and different plants in and around Bailey.

We were on our way to the place where the man had told us we could rent mountain bikes for a day of fun. On our ride up the mountain, we saw many small animals. Some of them were larger than usual and had crossed the bike trail in front of us. We saw huge rabbits, chipmunks and squirrels. Also a few gophers that stood on their back legs, watching us ride by.

By the time we had come back from our day of mountain biking, we were tired, but still had daylight left, so after we turned in the bikes, we drove away in the direction of our next adventure, in Arkansas. There would be another cave waiting for us to see.

We had driven for hours and crossed the Arkansas line. Our next stop to rest would be another campground surrounded by other people.

Diane and I had talked and were hoping that the tour bus was waiting there, so we could see Shawn and Sam again. When we pulled into our parking area, I looked around and it wasn't there. After a couple of hours, we agreed that they probably were a long ways away, in a different direction than the one that we had chosen for ourselves.

This campground had a food stand that the state park had installed. The man that ran it had hot dogs, hamburgers and even a soda bar. Diane and I bought a foot-long hot dog with the works, a bag of chips and a soda. Others were standing in line to do the same thing. In our mind we felt like this was pretty unique and out of the ordinary for a simple camping area.

We were approached by many visitors to the park that night and had made some new friends from different states and different parts of the world who were going north, south, east and west.

About 11:00 p.m. we all decided to go back to our camps and call it a day. Diane and I were almost asleep when we heard a huge roar. This not only startled us, but the other campers in the state park.

Everyone who didn't have a camper shell or RV climbed out of their tents and sleeping bags, grabbing their coolers, and ran to their vehicles.

It was a fairly good-sized bear that had smelled the odor of the food stand and trash cans, and had wandered into the park to see what he could find to eat.

This time we grabbed our sleeping bags and ran to my car as fast as we could, locking the doors as if the bear could open a door—which the next day we laughed about.

Because of this, it would mean another night of trying to get comfortable in my car and waking up to sore backs and necks. We laid awake, listening to all the surrounding noises and then went to sleep. That had been a day of not just seeing small animals, but one big one as well.

The next day when we woke up, we were on our way to see the Blanchard Spring Caverns. Even though we had taken our time this morning waking up and driving, we still made it there with some time to spare. Other people were lined up and ready to witness this wonder. It was a cave in Ozark-St. Francis National Forest. Inside of it were two levels that were open for guided tours. This cavern was known as the Half Mile Cave.

Like the other cavern that we had been in, we were amazed at what we had seen that day. After getting gas and something to eat, we were on our way to the great state of Texas. We had traveled a long ways with many miles to go before we reached our destination.

It was late afternoon and we had crossed the Texas

state line. We were driving on the Blue Bonnet Trail and also found a store that sold Blue Bonnet ice cream. We sat in my car, eating it, and talked about some good barbecue that we would eat for our supper that night.

It was time to stop again for the night, and in the morning we would continue our journey and go boating in the river. There was so much to see and do in Texas that on our way back we had planned on other stops, as we didn't want to miss out on anything.

We stayed in a small motel. There was a nice restaurant in the town that we were told served the best barbecue in Texas. The people in the restaurant were very nice, and the atmosphere was homey.

"Pat, I like this state," said Diane.

"Me too. I feel like at one time in my life I have been here before. Maybe when I was little I came here with my parents on one of our vacations," I replied.

"The people that live here are not only friendly, but helpful as well."

"They are," I agreed. "Maybe on our way back home we can spend more time here."

So after Diane and I agreed that Texas was at the top of our list, we finished our meal and went back to the motel room to prepare for the next day of fun and more wonderful Texas hospitality.

The next day we were up early and driving to the Blanco River to take in a morning of boating. It seemed again like our timing was perfect as we arrived at the spot just in time to pay the man in the booth and climb on board with the other tourists.

As we went down the river we saw once again a beautiful sight. The water was calm that day and bright blue. Everyone in the boat had on life jackets as did we, along with helmets. They, like us, kept taking pictures as we passed scenery that a lot of people dream about, but never get to experience. It was warm and a perfect day.

When we returned, it was still early afternoon and

we were ready to leave and drive close to where we would see the Inner Space Cavern.

— 3 —

Surprise Waiting

We knew that this would be an extraordinary tour that would leave us with questions and many hours of thought about what we saw that day.

As we drove up next to it, we had a few hours before they closed it. The caverns were carved by water, and were passing through limestone. There were prehistoric remains which fascinated us the entire way through. All of this Diane and I would be discussing for days to come. We were very impressed with what we had seen and it was time to leave.

Each day our adventures seemed to get better. In the morning we would be attending the State Fair and Rodeo. We had each bought a Western hat that we would wear for the occasion.

What we didn't know was that there would be a surprise there waiting for us. As we laid our heads down on our pillows in another campground that we had seen off the beaten path of the highway, we couldn't stop discussing the prehistoric remains that fascinated us. We had come a long way and were struggling to stay awake. It was late and we were once again asleep.

The next morning we woke up to beautiful stars and even though it was still very early, we wanted to make this a full day of fun. We were headed to see the biggest rodeo and fair in the world.

It was a warm day and time was of the essence, so we loaded my car and climbed in again to drive to where we wanted to be. When we arrived, we had to drive around some as the rodeo grounds were packed. As we paid and walked through the gate, we saw hundreds of people who had gotten there early like us, to partake in all the fun.

When we entered the gate, we saw a man with a cotton candy display. "Pat, let's stop. It isn't a fair without eating cotton candy," Diane commented.

"You are right. What flavor do you want to share, or do you want your own?" I asked, giggling.

"Let's get our own," Diane responded as she paid the man for a blue one.

I then paid him for a red one, and we walked away, nibbling on our choice of the day.

As we continued on, we saw roundabouts known as carousels and merry-go-rounds. There were other rides that had been set up for amusement. It was a carnival with not just different rides for the young and old, but also game stands that had been set up for people to win prizes. There were exhibits of livestock for competitions, also automobile racing, and something that we didn't expect. This would mean another encounter and visit with our new friends, Shawn and Sam.

We sat on chairs and listened to the group sing and play their musical instruments for hours. Shawn saw me sitting there and smiled at me. When they took a break, he set his guitar down on the stage and came over to me. Along with him came Sam, so he could talk to Diane.

"Pat, it is good to see you again. It's a small world," said Shawn.

"Yes, it is, and it is good to see you and Sam again," I replied as I smiled back at him.

"How long are you going to be here?" he asked.

"We will be here the whole day. How about you?"

"We will be playing for a couple more hours, and then won't play again until later. After we are done, do you and Diane want to hang out with us for a while?" Shawn asked.

"It would be fine with me. There is a lot to see here."

"Yes, and if you like, we can see it together," Shawn responded.

"We will sit here and wait for you to finish. Then we can walk around."

"That works for me, and I am sure Sam as well."

Break time was over. Shawn and Sam returned to the stage. We sat in our chairs and listened to their band until they were finished. Like before at the campground, they had drawn a crowd of people that continued to sit and listen to them.

After they took their bows and were done, they put their instruments in the tour bus and came back to where we were sitting. It was going to be an extra fun day.

Diane was happy to be spending some time with Sam, and as we walked away from the stage, we talked.

"You forgot to mention that you were going to be here," I said to Shawn.

"We have been here for a couple of days now. Today is our last day before we leave."

"Where do you girls want to go first?" Sam asked.

"Let's try the amusement park," Diane commented.

I looked at Shawn and he shook his head, letting us know that would be fine with him. It was fine with Sam, and so we walked in that direction.

"What do you want to ride first?" Shawn asked.

"Whatever you do," I replied.

We all agreed that the roller coaster would be the most fun, so we stood in line waiting to get on. Next we went to the tea cups, where Diane announced after the ride that she shouldn't have eaten the cotton candy. Of course, I had to laugh at her. We went on the Ferris wheel and the water slide, and just about everything else that they had there.

Our next walk was to the automobile show. There were old cars there that were like brand new, and we climbed the steps to the bleachers to watch the race car competition.

From there we went to the place where they had games. Shawn won me a bear, and Sam won Diane a stuffed doll. We continued to walk around until we came to a food court. It was time to eat.

"What would you like to eat, Pat?" Shawn asked.

"A burger, fries and a drink," I replied.

Shawn and Sam went to get food for all of us, and then as we sat there eating, we were talking even more.

"We hope that you will stay for our last performance tonight before we leave here," Shawn remarked.

I could see that Diane was having a great time with Sam, and I was enjoying Shawn's company as well, so I said, "Yes, Shawn, we will hang out with you as long as we can today and tonight, before you and the rest of your band leave here."

"That sounds great, Pat. I hope you are having a bunch of fun today."

"We are, and thank you. This place is amazing. We have been to county fairs, but nothing like this state fair."

"It is big and has a lot of people that attend it."

"The carnival rides were a huge attraction, and personally I loved the cars that raced."

We sat there and continued to talk and eat. Then Shawn said that it was a bunch of fun for him and he knew for Sam as well, and that they needed to get back to the bus for rehearsal and then later they would see us at the last concert.

We watched them walk away, and Diane and I continued our journey to see the livestock exhibits and the competition of other things. We had gotten to know Shawn and Sam better and were glad to see our new friends maybe one last time.

The day was starting to come to an end. We had watched the rodeo with the steer wrestling, saddle bronco riding, bareback bronco riding, bull riding and barrel racing. Now it was time to go back to the concert and watch

Shawn and Sam perform.

As we found a place to sit, Shawn and Sam looked out at us. Their performance was even better than before, and at that moment there was nowhere else we wanted to be. Again a huge crowd of people gathered to listen to every song they sang and played. It was getting late, and after a couple of hours, again everyone on stage was thanking us for listening and taking their last bows for the concert. The people were leaving, and Diane and I stayed there.

Shawn and Sam had set their instruments on the stage and came down to say goodbye.

"Thank you for watching, Pat. One of these days our paths will cross again. I have your phone number and you have mine. We will keep in touch, as I know Sam and Diane will," Shawn spoke.

"Yes, Shawn. We have some more of our scenic road trip to take, and then we will be going back to Bailey. Good luck with your concerts, and I will give you a call soon, to see where life is taking you," I responded.

Shawn gave me a hug and Sam also gave Diane one. Then they both turned around and went back on stage to put their instruments in the bus and get ready to move out of there for their next journey they were scheduled to take. Diane and I waved at them one last time, and walked away, headed to my car. It had been an interesting, exciting and fun day. The best part was seeing our musician friends again.

After we had left the parking area and were driving again, we agreed that it was too late to try to get a motel, so it would mean another night of camping.

We drove south and before long we had found a place to pull over for the night. We decided to sleep in the car again and avoid any animals that might wander upon us. Before long, we were dreaming about our adventures that we had already taken, and those to come.

— 4 —

More Adventures, But Questions

The next morning we saw a beautiful sunrise and had more fun waiting for us as we continued to drive south. We had the Buddy Holly Museum to see in Lubbock, Texas.

We drove for hours and then reached our destination. The city was huge and lots of people were driving around. When we found where we were going, we went inside the gift shop and paid for our small tour that was very interesting. We went into a room to watch a small clip of Buddy Holly, and then to another room to look at the artifacts and documents from his childhood. When we were done inside, we walked over to the house that had been restored. We were told that it was open to the public as well. Again we were excited and impressed.

When we left the city of Lubbock, going in the direction of Arizona, we thought that we had seen our last exciting moment until we returned. In the distance we saw something that resembled a small tornado. It was coming in our direction and so we kept driving. Soon it was upon us and had become a strong, well formed whirlwind. As it went across the highway in front of us, we knew we had seen our first dust storm. We watched as it kept going, getting bigger as it went. This was something that we had never witnessed before.

After many hours of driving, we were crossing the state line into New Mexico. We had a few more hours to go and we would be at our next stop of the day. This would be the Roswell Alien Museum that is very well known to many people.

We had eaten at a restaurant named "Charley's" and were on our way into town to see the museum before they closed the door. The museum was situated in a part of town where there was very little parking. That afternoon there were many cars around the area that the museum had provided, and Diane and I had to park about a half mile away in order to find a spot.

When we walked through the doors, we had about an hour to see what we could see before the museum would be closed for the day. After reading all the documentation that was there, it was up to us to decide whether or not we believed that aliens really did exist. This had happened on July 3, 1947, during a thunderstorm, and several people that were standing around were discussing their own opinions on whether it all was fact or fiction. As for Diane and myself, we read everything and stood around looking at each other, not knowing what to say.

Our first thought was whether or not it all was true, or just made up for entertainment. We were fascinated with everything the museum provided to look at, and after we left, we discussed our own points of view. It was amazing and we were once again happy that we had gone.

On our way back to catch the highway that would take us in the direction we needed to go, we passed another scenic spot that was called the Bottomless Lakes State Park. Some people were standing around it and it looked to us like they were planning on swimming that evening.

We wanted to see the Cathedral Rock, but because of it being so late in the day, and hours away, we decided to once more stop at a motel for the night.

Our adventure that day had been a long one and it wasn't long before we found a motel room where we went to bed to sleep.

Each day kept getting better and better, and it wouldn't be much longer and we would arrive at Long

Beach, which was our destination for this trip.

In the morning we were up and at it about an hour after waking up. It was just barely light out, but we still had a ways to go before we would be at our scenic place of beauty.

As we were driving, we saw many formations of rock that were standing tall and proud. Diane and I tried to make something out of each and every one of them. One rock formation reminded me of a castle, and another one reminded Diane of a side view of a man's head. We spent hours looking and talking.

When we did arrive at Cathedral Rock, there were a bunch of people standing around, taking photographs of it. It was quite a sight to see. It was a red bed of sandstone that had been formed from coastal sand dunes. We walked around for a couple of hours, looking at everything. This was a sight that also would be etched in our memories of this trip.

We were not far from the Grand Canyon and wanted to make the best out of our day. We kept driving and once we had gotten to it, it was another miracle that was created. It was huge. The sides were steep in the canyon, and we were told that this had been carved by the Colorado River. Also, the tour guide said that some caves had been inhabited by the Pueblo Native American Indians, who had considered it to be a holy site. There was so much beauty to see, and a long ways down to the bottom of it.

After the tour was over, we were once again driving southwest. We wanted to get to Long Beach as we had so much to see and do there as well. We kept going until we started getting closer and had crossed the state line into California.

We were so excited to get to our destination, we didn't sleep. After a while, we could smell the ocean and knew that we had made it to the place we wanted to be for the rest of our journey, until we had to go a different route back home in a week.

As we pulled into a hotel in Long Beach, we were ready to sleep for a few hours before we woke up and went further into the city to take our boat ride to the Catalina Island that was like Paradise on Earth. This was something that we had heard was one of the most beautiful sights in the world.

When we walked into the hotel, there was a man at the front door who stood there watching everything that Diane and I did. Somehow he made us feel uncomfortable, but as tired as we were, we didn't care as long as we made it to our room that we had reserved.

Our room was very nice, and it wasn't long and we were in our beds and fast asleep.

When we woke up, it was dark and our day was gone except for walking to the elevator to take it down to the first floor, where we needed to be, and to a restaurant close by.

Again this same man was at the door and he kept staring at us, and Diane said she wanted to walk up to him and ask him what his problem was, but I talked her out of it. I had to laugh at her, though.

One thing about a city in California is that no matter what time of the day or night, there is always something happening there and places open to eat at.

We found a place and made our way back to the hotel, and back to bed. It would be an early morning and a complete day of fun on the island.

The next day we were expecting to leave our room. When Diane tried to open the door, it wouldn't open. It was locked. This was something that we didn't like, and we needed answers.

I picked up the phone and called the hotel operator, to inform them that we were stuck in our room.

The phone rang several times and then I heard, "Operator."

"Yes, this is Pat Morris. My friend and I are stuck in

our room and the door won't open," I said firmly.

"There is a reason for that, madam. We have a man with a gun that is loose in here, and we are trying to keep our guests safe."

"How long is it going to take before the man is caught and we are unlocked from our room?" I asked.

"We are not sure, madam. We have called the police department and they are on their way. Stay away from your door," she warned.

"We will," I said.

I then had to explain to Diane what was going on. Diane didn't do well under pressure, so this was going to be quite interesting.

"Diane, stay away from the door. The hotel has locked us in here because there is a man in the hotel that has a gun. Stay calm as the police department has been called," I told her.

"You are kidding me, Pat! We could check in, but can't check out if we want to," she said.

"That's right," I said.

We heard noises up and down the hallway outside our door, but stayed across the room and away from the door.

Hours went by and we were still stuck in there with no food, and no way of getting out, short of climbing out the window of a huge hotel and walking along the edge to another room, where we hoped the window would be open and we could escape in some way. Even with all this going on, we knew that wasn't going to happen, and it was time to just sit down and hope the mystery was solved soon and we could leave here and find a different hotel or motel to stay in.

Still more hours went by, and so I picked up the phone to call the downstairs operator. This time all the phone did was ring and no one answered. I even got so desperate that I was going to call my dad and tell him what was going on. I tried, but couldn't get an outside line, so all we could do was wait this out.

Our thoughts were that maybe it was that strange man at the door who kept watching us.

"Diane, you don't know what I would give right now to be face to face with that bear in the campground," I said, giggling.

"I know, Pat. We were so afraid that night, and now we are being held captive in a hotel room. Our road trip was great, and this must have been the danger that our parents were referring to when they were trying to talk us out of doing this," Diane said, also giggling.

"I looked out the window and didn't see any police cars coming or going away from here. Why do you think that is?" Diane asked.

"I don't know. That is very strange. By now they should have caught the guy and taken him to jail," I remarked.

Again I called the operator and the phone rang and rang. Now I was starting to get nervous and wondered if Diane and I were going to be stuck in that room until someone discovered us days from now. Did they forget about us?

"Could this be a practical joke, Pat?" Diane asked.

"If it is, it isn't funny," I responded with some anger to my voice.

"What do we do now?" Diane asked.

"Sit back and wait, I guess. If someone doesn't unlock our door in a few hours, we are going to start screaming and will draw attention from someone," I said.

"Do you think that is a good idea?" Diane asked.

"Not really, but the operator won't answer the phone. I can't call my dad, and we are really going to be hungry before long."

"I agree with you, but what happens if we start screaming, and the man with the gun is walking up and down the hallway and hears us, then shoots the door down to get to us? I think we need to give it a little longer, Pat,"

Diane remarked.

Who would have guessed that Diane, out of the two of us, would be the logical one? She was right. I sat there, snickering to myself.

More time went by and we heard nothing outside the door and no police sirens. Nor did we see any lights from police cars on the street. This was very annoying and I had enough of it.

"Be prepared, Diane. We are going to start screaming from the top of our lungs. I can't take this wait any longer. We didn't travel this far to sit in the room for hours or days. This is too mysterious for me."

So Diane and I screamed our heads off and there was still no response. I picked up the phone and again, no operator answered the phone. There was nothing that we could do but sit and try to wait this out. Whoever it was that had a gun had every one of the staff either held hostage, or they had run out of the hotel and gone home, which was where Diane and I wished we were right now.

"Pat, when we decided to take this trip, we had made up our minds that we were coming, no matter what happened. Along the way we saw things that we only dreamed about for years. This, I agree, was not on the list of fun when we checked in and can't check out. But it is what it is right now. We can't let this ruin all the fun that we have had, and there has to be an explanation for all of this," said Diane.

Her words of wisdom made sense, and so we went in the room where our beds were and laid down to sleep. Maybe everything would look better in the morning, when it was light outside again. Even if we screamed out the window now as it had turned dark, no one below would see us.

The next morning, when we woke up, we were going to make it a good day. We would get out of our room, no matter what it took.

I went to the phone and dialed the operator. With

once again no response, Diane and I opened the window in our room. We started yelling again, and a man down below heard us.

"Are you all right up there?" he asked.

"No! We are trapped in our room, and no one in the lobby will answer the phone. Can you help us?" I asked.

"Sure, I'll try," he replied.

"Please do, as we need to get out of here!" I responded.

We watched as the man walked in the direction of the entrance to the hotel, and then he walked back and yelled up to us, "What room are you in?"

"We are in Room 612."

He then walked again to the entrance of the hotel. It was within minutes and we saw the door open to our room. How had he done this?

"Now you can leave. The lady at the desk told me that last night they unlocked your door."

"What kind of a hotel is this?" I said.

"I don't know, but you are free to leave now," the man responded.

Feeling stupid again because we didn't check the door before yelling out the window, we decided that even though we were planning on staying for a week here, we changed our minds and it was time to check out. This was *not* where we wanted to be.

After grabbing our suitcases, we left the room and ran down the stairs to the front desk. Standing there was a lady. With what we had just been put through, we had questions and we weren't leaving until they all were answered.

"Why and how did you forget about us?" I asked.

"The man that had the gun was on the same floor as you. We had undercover police officers here that softly walked up to his room and brought him out about 2 a.m. You must have been sleeping at that time. We unlocked your door after that. Our phone lines haven't been working, and we couldn't call you. Do you want to continue to stay here?" she asked.

"No. This has been a big mystery to us, and it is not the hotel that we thought it would be. I know this probably isn't your fault, but it is pretty sad when a person can check in, but can't check out whenever they choose to, even if it is at 2 a.m.," I spoke in a firm tone.

"We will be happy to help you with your luggage, if you like," the lady responded.

Of course the answer was no again. Diane and I left the hotel, headed in the direction of my car.

Our fun and adventure turned into a road block for a couple of days, but we found a regular motel where we could climb out the window if this ever happened again. We took our time picking it out, though.

In Long Beach we continued to witness the beautiful lights of the city, the smell of the ocean, the beach and the friendly people walking around. We also took in a movie.

We had gone to Catalina Island many times, as one day there wasn't enough. The tour of the *Queen Mary* was spectacular, and after our week there was up, it was time for us to leave and return to Bailey.

As for Shawn and Sam, we saw them once again in a small town called St. George, Utah. After a third time of being in the same place at the same time, we all were convinced that all of us were destined to keep in touch with one another.

Within a year after we arrived home, Diane married Sam. They moved to Texas and lived in a city that Diane had grown to love. It wasn't long before they added a new member to their family. It was a baby girl, whom they named Austin. Sam had quit the band as had Shawn.

Shawn had been offered a really good job with a law firm not far from Bailey. I had put my college years to use and got a job at a hospital not far from where Shawn lived. We continued to see each other and maybe someday we might get married as well.

Diane would always be my best friend, no matter

where we lived, and we would have many times to discuss our road trip to California. What we had seen along the way was outstanding, and if we hadn't taken the chance of going on this adventure, we wouldn't have met Shawn nor Sam.

We also talked about the big hotel and the man with the gun that kept us locked in our room for a couple of days. Diane and I laughed at ourselves for not checking the door first that morning, before screaming out the window and involving a man off the street. With all of this, we both agreed that it is sad when anyone can check in, but can't check out.

Would we do it all again? Of course we would.

Other Books by Jana Nolan

THE OLD HENDERSON MINE

MIND POWER

SOUNDS OF FEAR

SECRETS OF SLEEPING INDIAN MOUNTAIN

PURE VENGEANCE

Visit her Author Web site at
JanaNolan.com